"Intense and lyrical, Heather Duffy Stone's story about transformations wrenches the heart and then puts it back together again, stronger and better for havi~~~~ book."

Friend~~~~ ~~ove,
and unexpected secrets

Nadio and his twin sister, Noelle, always had a unique bond. And somehow, Keeley Shipley fit perfectly into their world. But when Keeley spends the summer in England, she comes home changed, haunted by a dark memory. As she and Nadio fall in love, they try to hide it from Noelle, who's jealously guarding a secret of her own. Slowly, a lifelong friendship begins to crack under the crushing weight of past trauma, guarded secrets, jealousy, obsession... and an unexpected love that could destroy them.

For Luke.
Not my twin but my brother and my mirror.

This Is What I Want to Tell You

Heather Duffy Stone

Woodbury, Minnesota

First Edition
First Printing, 2009

Book design by Steffani Sawyer
Cover design by Lisa Novak
Cover image © 2008 by image100/Alamy

Flux, an imprint of Llewellyn Publications

Library of Congress Cataloging-in-Publication Data
Duffy-Stone, Heather, 1977–
  This is what I want to tell you / Heather Duffy-Stone.—1st ed.
     p. cm.
  ISBN 978-0-7387-1450-9
  [1. Interpersonal relations—Fiction. 2. Best friends—Fiction.
3. Friendship—Fiction. 4. Brothers and sisters—Fiction.
5. Twins—Fiction.] I. Title.
  PZ7.D878148Th 2009
  [Fic]—dc22
                                    2008044040

Flux
Llewellyn Publications
A Division of Llewellyn Worldwide, Ltd.
2143 Wooddale Drive, Dept. 978-0-7387-1450-9
Woodbury, MN 55125-2989, U.S.A.
www.fluxnow.com

Printed in the United States of America

Acknowledgments

Writing is in many ways a solitary act, but there are some people without whom this book would never have happened.

Hillery Stone is not just a poet, brilliant in her own right, of a brilliant lineage, but she has also been my best friend since we were eleven and my tireless supporter, critic, reader, and right hand in the telling of this story, and all stories.

Elissa Haden Guest wrote a book called *Over the Moon* that I read when I was twelve or so, and I've wanted to write this book ever since. She remains an inspiration.

Darci Manley has been with this book since Parker had a different name and all along she has pushed me harder, pulled me forward, and flooded me with the details and inspirations that made this book whole. Micol Ostow and every one of my MB writer friends also brought this story from an idea to a reality.

I wrote much of this book after returning to New York from Rome. The students I taught in Rome—the reluctant members of my English Comp class—inspired me to tell this story; in part, it belongs to them. My friends and colleagues there, and especially my roommates, gave me the belief in possibility that let me think this book could happen.

Of course, I thank teachers, peers, friends, and editors—lifelong supporters of my writing who believed this was possible long before I ever did. My Tribe, especially.

Andrew Karre, who weathered my neurotic ramblings and guided this manuscript into the kind of book it could be with his brilliant vision and an absolute understanding of my intentions. Jenoyne Adams, who came to me through dozens of fortuitous connections and advocated tirelessly on my behalf to bring this book to you.

My sister-in-law Braeden Stone, who said to me, "I don't know how you do it, but you write the things I felt yet didn't know how to express when I was a teenager." This is the greatest compliment I've received yet.

My father, who always let me be a writer and pushes me still to be everything else he thinks I can be, who reminds me that I can do all of it. And Deb, who always has faith. Aunt Karen, who never made me walk too far and taught me to appreciate the finest things.

My mom. Who is my other half. She is the strength and power in everything I do. And everything I write is because she told me I could.

Noelle

I can't tell you exactly what happened, but I can tell you part of it.

My part.

I once read that you should always write about what you know, that what you know will tell the best story. What I know now is that the stories people tell are always about our insecurities, about the things we left behind, and about the things we wish we could do again. The real story isn't about what you know; it's about what you wish you knew then.

The story I want to tell leaves some stuff out, because

to tell all of it is too true. And some stuff needs to be kept secret.

Here is something true. I met him at a party. His name was Parker. The party was at Jessica Marino's older brother's loft in the city. It was loud and dim and dirty, the way lofts are in your imagination. Jessica and I both wore black eyeliner smudged in thick clouds around our lashes and tore our tank tops into jagged pointy Vs. Jessica's brother mostly ignored us and we hung in the corners of the room, trying, without admitting it, to make our faces pout and suggest, like all of the faces we saw around us, like all of these faces who seemed older and better and barely noticed us.

I saw Parker when he came in; he was taller than everyone else and wore a black hat tilted low over the left side of his face. He swaggered. He knew people. His eyes pierced even from far away.

He looked like everything I wasn't.

The whole room was dirty and a little bit faded. I felt like I wasn't supposed to be there. I felt like in that moment I wanted to be the kind of girl that he'd want to talk to. I felt like I wanted to be a rock star.

Then it happened. He started talking to me. He came up to me when Jessica was in the bathroom and I was hugging the perimeter of the room.

Hey, he said, and it felt like I was dreaming.

He asked me who I knew. Up close his eyes were cold-water blue. Everything about him was long and lean. He was wearing a black T-shirt and right here in front of me I could see it was faded and thin and his shoulders pushed through it, straining the thin fabric. His hair was a million kinds of brown—pushed up on one side like he'd been sleeping, or like the hat, now gone and forgotten, had shaped the hair it left exposed.

He asked me where I was from and I said something about Jessica's brother and I wondered why he was still talking to me.

Damn, you're beautiful, he said. I saw you right when I walked in. What's your name?

Noelle, I whispered.

No-Elle, he said, and I watched his tongue pause against the back of his teeth at the end of my name. It had never sounded like that before.

No-Elle, he repeated, as if it were something different. As if it were his.

I can't even tell you, that feeling when someone calls
you pretty, your whole face feels hot and then the rest
of your body gets hot and then everything around you
turns blurry.

How come I've never seen you before, he said.

And I knew he was older but it suddenly occurred to
me that he wasn't that much older. And that I had him
completely fooled. That all of it, everything, was in my
hands. I'd never felt that way before. I leaned my head
to the side so a piece of hair fell over my eye.

*   *   *

The thing I need to tell you is that before this night,
Keeley Shipley was my best friend. All summer she'd
been away from home. I got a job that summer at the
Cree-Mee stand and I worked with Jessica Marino. I
knew Jessica from school where she wore black eyeliner
and corduroy miniskirts and seemed to know a secret
that nobody else in Geometry knew. She was the kind
of person who makes you feel like there is a whole other

4

life out there and it is way better than the one you are living. That summer I rode around in Jessica's car after work and we smoked joints and felt bored and waited for something to happen. The whole time I couldn't shake the feeling that something was happening in Keeley's life and it had nothing to do with me.

Keeley was my first friend—besides Nadio, my twin brother. We had this thing that a lot of kids don't have—this connection where we just got each other. Like we were meant to be friends. For ten years the only person who understood anything about me was Keeley Shipley. For most of those ten years I didn't even notice how our lives were different. How her sweeping house on the hill shadowed ours. How she was so beautiful everyone just stared at her. How everything near her seemed to turn the color gold—really. But the thing was, the thing that made it all okay, was that Keeley never seemed to notice any of this either. But then she went away. Then she started to live this whole life outside of our life. Then my brother Nadio and Keeley Shipley fell in love and that was the end of everything I knew.

The night I met Parker, Keeley and Nadio weren't in love yet, but I think I knew it was coming. The night I met Parker was the last real night of the summer. The night I met Parker I was almost the same age as our mother was when she bought a one-way ticket to Italy and met our father on an overnight train. The night I met Parker was the night Keeley was coming home; but when Jessica called me and asked me to go to this party with her, it was like I just knew I had to go. I didn't leave Keeley a message or anything, I just went. Like I forgot that was the night she was coming home.

Except I never forgot.

My brother only remembers a photograph of the three of us meeting, but I remember the real first time I saw Keeley. She had pale, pale skin and millions of freckles and I thought her face was the most amazing thing I had ever laid eyes on—so many tiny painted freckles, and white-blonde hair—it turned gold as we got older but that first day it was almost white. Keeley didn't hide behind her parents the way other kids did around us. She was never intimidated by the fact that there were two of us. She just walked right in, and she fit.

Before that summer everything was quiet. Everything was Nadio and me and Keeley, everything was the orchard where we lived and the hiking trails around us and our bikes along the road and sleeping in between our houses in tents. Through sophomore year, most of the time it was like we had the world to ourselves. Then Keeley flew to England for the summer and Nadio started running all the time and Jessica Marino started to drive me around in her car. That world we'd had to ourselves wasn't there anymore. There was a whole new one.

When I met Parker I thought I could make him fill in all those spaces and gaps that my brother and Keeley left behind, even though the shapes were all wrong. I'd never seen anyone like him—no one like him had ever paid attention to me.

He had tattoos. Not just a few but a lot. Up and down his arms and across his shoulder blades. I only saw some of them that first night, but I could see their points and edges beneath the sleeves and above the neck of his shirt. I tried not to stare.

Hey, it's okay, he said. Look at them.

And he turned his arms over and pointed at them and told me where he was when he got each one—it was like a whole history of his life, right there on his skin, carved in with needles and ink and painting him from one place to the next. And there were so many places.

My first one, he said about a huge Celtic symbol on his right shoulder. I got this one in Boston when I was visiting my cousin. You know, Celtic warriors used the art on their bodies to intimidate their enemies.

I didn't know that.

On the back of his hand, a symbol that looked like swiftly painted lines. He put his palm down on my thigh and that tattooed hand was framed by my jeans, his fingers sending chills through the fabric.

It's the Chinese symbol for fire, he said, nodding down at his hand. You know, its warmth, its danger all at once, and it's my—you know you need fire to cook, and that's what I do.
You cook? I asked. I could barely concentrate.
Yeah, he said.

He turned his hand, lifting his fingers from my jeans, letting the breath out. On the inside of his wrist a spiral starting small, wound tight at the veins at his wrist and then unwinding, snaking all the way up to the inside of his elbow. A serpent.

You know, temptation, he said.

He had a tattoo that ran in a column down his spine— it said
what
does not
destroy me
makes me
stronger
in straight, black heavy script.

What almost destroyed you? I asked him.

But that was later. That was a different night. I didn't see the one on his back that first night.

*   *   *

My brother and I are telling this story because we realized that it wasn't one story, but two. For the first time, the things that happened to us looked so different. Even Keeley, who had always been there in both of our eyes, suddenly became two different people. I always thought

I was the only one who knew who she was exactly, but last year I realized I didn't really know who anyone was—Keeley, Nadio, much less me.

Keeley had been in England all summer and the night she got home, I wasn't there. I was meeting Parker. She and I had never been apart for more than a few days, not since we were five years old. But what was I supposed to do? Was I supposed to just sit and wait for her all summer?

Nadio

It is hard to picture what last summer felt like. I know I was someone else then and I probably couldn't have imagined who I'd become—who we'd all become—but now that I know, part of me wants to remind myself what it was like before. I told Noelle about the way I'd written to our father, on invisible pages but with permanent ink. We need to do that, she said, we need to tell this story, even if the pages are invisible.

Before, I only knew Keeley as an extension of my sister. She was the blonde half to Noelle's brown—they were like daytime and nighttime—each in need of the other one but living as perfect opposites. Keeley was the quiet part and Noelle was the bold part. That was how I saw them. I knew Keeley in a way that didn't tell her and my sister apart, like each of them was only who she was with the other one. But the night she came home from her summer in Oxford, that night I couldn't even see how they had fit together. Suddenly, that night, Keeley was all her own.

I always thought I remembered the first time I saw her, but Noelle says I'm remembering a photograph and not the actual meeting. She says the photo was taken later, after we knew each other, but I can't help wondering who took it; Lace never thought to take pictures, she wasn't that kind of mother, and I'd never seen the Shipleys with a camera. Maybe they really did watch Keeley grow up, or maybe there never was a photograph. Noelle just tells me there was one; I've never seen it. What I remember is a darkened entryway in the Shipleys' living room, the white border of the doorway framing Keeley and my sister—my sister in an orange dress and Keeley in a green dress—and they were laughing and reaching out to each other. I was in the background. I was the same color as the carpet. I was watching them.

I've lived at the bottom of the orchard my whole life. The place where we live is strange in a dozen ways. For one, we live in the gatehouse of a sort of run-down estate. There is no such thing as a groundskeeper for the estate, though that was probably who lived in our house once. It belongs to the college now, and the big house and its land always goes to the chair of the Languages and Literature department. Our mom has worked in the college bookstore since before we were born, and a long time ago the chair of the Lit department saw her carrying me and my sister and two bags of groceries up the porch steps of her apartment near campus and said, why don't you move into the gatehouse? There's a lot of land, it's great for kids, and it sits empty. We were living there when he retired and Keeley's dad moved in to take his place, but the Shipleys wanted us to stay and even asked our mom to help take care of Keeley. To me, this land has always felt like all of ours, although later I realized my sister didn't feel that way.

It's strange here too, because in the orchard there is absolute silence, far from everything. Down the hill is the village, where the college claims square houses and brick buildings and a public high school pulls together handfuls of students from spread-out small towns. But if I run far enough, to the end of the orchard, I can see the dim tired landscape of the city. Our teachers and the Shipleys always talk about how the city was once this great industrial capital, but now it isn't much more than boarded-up windows and gray streets. If I get on a sputtering public bus from the college, I can ride it into the city and walk the spray-painted sidewalks to a few cafés and restaurants and a record store and tall buildings with filmy glass windows. All of these businesses look a little scared to me—their polished windows cowering in between broken glass and plywood.

In the orchard, we're sort of perched between gatehouse and big house, city and country … but even the country is on the brink of being bigger, and even the city is basically on the edge of falling apart.

Sometimes I feel like I know the orchard better in the dark than in the daylight. That summer I started running at night; there was always some light from the stars, but I didn't need it. I could feel the ground almost better than I could see the path. The field sloped gradually down to the first row of trees and then, once I entered that first row, I'd hold my arms out, falling a little bit, pushing off from one tree to the next. After I ran, I'd rest, leaning against the crumbling edge of the stone wall—the stone was cool and smooth. I loved this part of night—the darkest part. Some people were scared of it. Some kind of light always filtered through, some kind of sound always reminded you that life was moving around you. Sometimes I'd feel around me for a stone or a twig and throw it deeper into the woods, just to wake up, just to connect to something.

That's where I was the night Keeley came in. She brushed through a break in the trees and then she was just standing there, like she'd been standing there all along, a long heavy brown sweater wrapped around her. The sweater was thick and old, but inside it she looked leaner and smoother and—different—like someone I was just meeting for the first time. She smiled. She held her hand out then she dropped it.

Hi, she said.
Hi. I took a step forward.
How was your summer?

I looked at her. It took me a minute to realize she'd said something. It took me longer to realize what it was. A piece of hair fell over her eyes, longer and lighter than I remembered.

Oh, it was good. Fine.

She smiled. Her smile was always easy. She pulled her hands inside her sleeves.

Which?
Which what?
Good or fine?

Was she being funny? I tried to smile.

Good. Good, I said.

She pushed her hair behind her ears. She moved closer, sitting down slowly on the stone wall. I turned. I was standing over her now.

And Noelle? she asked.
You haven't seen her yet?
Well, I came to see her. She gestured behind her without looking. But then I saw you.

She paused.

And I wanted to say hi.

She couldn't have seen me. It was dark. I was deep into the orchard. But I didn't want to think about that.

Oh, she's good. She's … she'll be really happy to see

you. I'm not sure where she is but, you know, she's really good. She's been working at the ice cream place.

I couldn't sit down. I pressed my foot back and forth, heel toe, pushing the mud down.

I could tell Keeley didn't believe me.

Will you sit down with me? She patted the wall next to her.

Okay, I said. I sat.

You look good. She looked at me sideways. What did you do all summer?

Oh, I ran.

There was something about her voice. It was like she'd gone away and then she'd come back with some completely other person inside her skin.

She smiled, laughing a little with her lips closed.

From what?

Oh no, I—I stopped.

She was making a joke. She was joking. What was wrong with me?

Me too, she said. I ran every morning—there are

all of these fields in Oxford, grazing cows and every-thing. It made me feel less homesick. Maybe we can run together some time?

How was your summer? I'd forgotten to ask.

She turned away and brought her sleeves up to her face. She stood up and walked back to the line of trees.

It was summer.

Suddenly, I didn't want her that far away. It was like the air between us was getting thinner and thinner. All of my muscles and joints were heavy, burrowing into the mud, my skin didn't fit, I couldn't move. Suddenly, I couldn't move.

She turned around.

Are you coming back up to the house?

I could feel the mud around my feet. My hands on the cold wall.

She tilted her head.

Nadio?

I couldn't move.

She looked at me for another second. Then she came back toward me. She knelt down in front of me and pushed her hands down on my thighs. She leaned in. This was a girl I didn't know. Who was she? She pressed on my thighs until I could feel my feet and started to move them. She kept pressing until my feet and legs and hands came back to life. She kept pressing and looking at me with her hair over her eyes. I lifted my hands up and put them on either side of her face. She breathed against my hands and closed her eyes. I leaned in and kissed her.

Noelle

I don't know what happened with my brother that summer. I wish I could explain it. It was like, from the very day Keeley left, we didn't know what to do with each other.

Do you want to do the Snake Mountain hike? he asked me at the beginning of the summer, the Saturday after she left. We always did the Snake Mountain hike. Lace would pack us granola bars and Keeley would make mozzarella sandwiches and Nadio would carry it all in his backpack.

But I didn't. I didn't feel like hiking.

So we rode our bikes into town and got iced coffees and

drank them on the porch of the Coyote Café, but we didn't have anything to say. We sat on the porch, our legs hanging over the edge, plastic cups sweating in our hands, and I looked down: four feet encased in black Converse, and all of a sudden his feet were bigger, his feet were unfamiliar.

I'm gonna see about getting a job at the Cree-Mee stand, I said. I'd never thought about getting a job but right then I knew I needed one.

Okay, he said.

He looked over at our bikes, tied to the post office fence. It looked funny, two bikes tangled awkwardly. We were too old for bikes anyway. Young for our grade, we had to wait until we turned sixteen in October to take our driving test, but we were still too old for bikes.

I'm gonna go for a run, he said.

He kicked his feet to the ground and started toward his bike. He turned around. I was still sitting on the porch.

Hey, Nole. Tonight let's go get a pizza.

Okay, I said. I felt relieved.

But we never got a pizza. I got a job at the Cree-Mee stand

that morning and started work right away. After work, Jessica Marino invited me to get a pizza. Then she gave me a ride home. We left my bike tied to the post office fence.

The night Keeley came home, I know part of me felt like it wasn't fair that she'd left me and had this whole life. Now I'm sorry I wasn't there. But I'm not sorry I met Parker.

By the time I came back from the party that night, everyone was asleep. There were no lights on in our house or hers, and I was floating on the feeling of Parker's fingertips on my thigh.

The next morning Keeley came down the hill for breakfast. When I came downstairs, she was already sitting at the table with Lace and Nadio. Lace was standing over her slicing a peach into her cereal bowl, one sliver at a time, like she did when we were kids, like Keeley couldn't hold a knife herself. Nadio was sitting on the other side of the table with his chin on his hands. Nadio and Lace were both staring at Keeley like she'd said something amazing. Both of their eyes were fixed on her. No one heard me come in. I don't even think anyone was talking.

Hi, I said.

Keeley looked up. She was wearing her running shorts and a man's T-shirt and her hair was in a ponytail. It looked blonder—she looked blonder. I mean she was lighter somehow. I can't explain it.

She stared at me for a second and then she jumped up.

Noelle!

She hugged me. I could already feel there was something there, something like cold air between us. I hugged her back and then we both pulled away and looked at each other. Lace and Nadio watched us.

Well? I said.
Where were you last night? she said at the same time.
I was out. I'm sorry. I just totally forgot last night was the night...
I sent you like three texts before I got on the plane, she said.
I know, my phone—but I couldn't even finish.

Nadio was glaring at me.

It's okay. I'm just happy to see you.

I can drive you all into town, Lace said quietly. To buy—what do you need for school?

Thanks, Mom, Nadio said.

It felt strange, everybody involved in Keeley's coming home. She was my best friend. Now everybody was standing around, watching us, trying to make plans for us.

I need a new bag, I said.

Keeley looked relieved.

Wait, she said. I can drive!

Keeley had gotten her license just before she went to Oxford. But she'd never had a chance to drive us anywhere. I felt like something was left out of this moment— that the feeling of us driving somewhere, not being driven, should have felt bigger than it did.

Okay, I said.

Great, she said. Lemme just go get some money from my parents.

I'm gonna get dressed, I said.

Nadio stood up.

I'll go get my wallet, he said.

We all turned.

What? he said. I need notebooks.

I should have known then. We did stuff together, always had. But not shopping. Not on Keeley's first day back.

In the car, Nadio sat in the back seat and I sat in the front with Keeley. I watched her hands. She looked like she'd always been driving. That was how she was, I thought then, everything was natural for her. It was that way when Lace taught us how to ride bikes. Lace taught us all those things when we were little and Keeley's parents were working and Keeley, some days, would have breakfast, lunch and dinner at our house. One day after peanut-butter-and-honey sandwiches, we all followed Lace out to the dirt driveway. There was one bike, it must have been Keeley's, and I pedaled, terrified and wobbling, Lace gripping the back of the seat, and when she let go I just crashed onto my side. But with Keeley, Lace never even held on to the seat. She steadied the bike and Keeley clamped her feet on the pedals and suddenly she was moving, away from us. The three of us watched her pumping her legs up the driveway, upright, no hands, no training wheels. Natural.

Keeley was wearing brown boots and a loose white skirt. I'd never seen her wear anything like that before.

You never wrote back to any of my emails, she whispered. Then she giggled.

I know, I said. I could never sit down long enough to type—you know I was working.

I know, she said. She looked straight ahead.

I turned up the radio.

I tried to go online, I said. Every time I went on, you weren't there.

The time difference . . . Her voice trailed off.

She blinked and looked at me, smiling, and quickly turned back to the road.

Anyway, now I'm back! Something in her voice seemed wrong.

What did you DO all summer? she whispered.
Nothing, hung out. You know.

I couldn't figure out why I felt mad at her.

Nadio

I left before anyone was up. I left Lace a note and I left Noelle the last bowl of cereal and I biked to school. Lace would quietly fold up the note and save it somewhere, in a drawer or a box of hideous handmade Christmas ornaments or something labeled *Boo's first day of school notes*.

She calls me Boo.

She says I was scared of everything until I was five years old. The truth is, I still let her call me Boo as long as no one else is around.

Noelle won't even know I left her the last bowl of cereal. She won't know I ate the end piece of a stale loaf of bread. But I feel better anyway. I know what it is I feel guilty about, but if something as little as cereal helps, well, whatever works.

It took me just under twenty minutes to bike to school, and it was still cool enough that the wind felt good on my face and my fingertips got chilled. At school the sun burned an early morning hole just over the track, where I tied my bike to the fence and ran exactly nine laps. By the time I was done, my sweat felt like a second skin. It was all I could do to breathe. It wasn't so cool anymore. It was straight up, middle-of-summer hot. With every lap I took I'd tried to make what I was thinking about be anything other than Keeley. Than my sister. Than both of them in the same brain. It was just too weird.

I started writing to him in my head that morning, before I put ink to paper.

Dear Dario,
It's the first day of junior year. Not that this first day is any different from any other. What I mean is, you've never been here. The concept of missing you isn't something I can really say I get. The concept of having a father and then not having one isn't something I know. But I've found myself thinking what it would be like if I could ask you about these

things—about Molly from last year or what to do when my mom and sister seem kind of crazy or now—about Keeley. I'm supposed to be a man but I can't help thinking no one ever showed me what that is supposed to look like. That maybe that is why I ride the middle all the time—never offending anyone, never getting a hard time, but never much standing out either. For a long time we blamed you for anything that seemed bad in our family—my sister and I did. But now I'm starting to think that blame gives you too much credit. Anyway, you're not here to deny or defend so what's the point.

* * *

I walked my bike into the school lot and locked it to the still-empty rack. I crossed through the basketball court, filling up now with early morning players. I nodded a few greetings and a lot of the faces nodded back. It was the first day of school and there wasn't anyone I was looking for and there wasn't anyone I was afraid of. It had always been that way. I kind of slid through the rules, and that was fine with me.

I found I was all good as long as I stayed on the cross-country team. I could do all of the socially unacceptable academic things I wanted—honor roll and debating and Model U.N. and Literary Mag, slipping under the social radar as long as I was a runner. I could walk that line.

Plus, you're good-looking, Noelle said last spring.

Was I? I believed her. The way it was with Noelle and me, we said what the other couldn't see or admit—we never bullshitted. We couldn't. We shared the same instincts.

After Noelle said that, I started to notice the way some of the girls looked at me, like I could have gone up to any one of them and started talking and maybe even invited her to a movie or whatever and it would be okay. She'd probably say yes and it would all be pretty easy.

But nothing about that appealed to me. All I'm saying is, I didn't feel like hanging out with some girl who had nothing to say, who was boring as hell, just because I could.

The locker room was empty. Anyone who was in school this early was on the basketball court. After I took a shower I left my running clothes in my locker and went out to the courtyard. It was filling up now, a lot of yelling and shrieking and high-fiving and hand-shaking and awkward standing around. I made a beeline for the Class of '76 oak tree and sat under it and took out my book. I was still reading *Walden*, which Lace had given me over the summer. The thing is, it bored the hell out of me and half the time I wanted Henry David Thoreau to shut up and relax a little bit. But there were two things that kept me reading.

1. It was my dad's book. That's a long story, but having a book that had been in his hands, that said Dario Avelli in scratchy faded-black ink on the inside cover, a name he'd written when he was maybe just a little bit older than me, inside a book he'd carried around with him and given to maybe the first girl he'd loved, all of that made me unable to stop reading it.

2. The truth is, even with all the rambling that sometimes drove me to nodding off, I was kind of into the ideas HDT was talking about. The idea of isolating yourself from everything so you could understand it better. That part I could get.

Hey, you.

I looked up. Keeley was standing over me. It was hard to see her—the sun came down the back of her, gold where her hair was and green where her sweater was, and the front of her was dark, shadowed.

Hey. I closed the book.

You totally left me, Noelle said, standing behind her.

Hey. I stood up. I'm sorry, I wanted to run before ...

Whatever, Noelle said. Listen, I need to find Jessica. K, are you coming? Do you wanna just see me in Chem?

Noelle was already walking away.

Okay, Keeley said. I didn't know if she was talking to me or Noelle.

Hi, I said again. I felt ridiculous.

Noelle is being so weird with me. It's like she knows. How could she know?

Keeley was talking about it out loud now. That made it real. I'd kissed Keeley Shipley.

She doesn't know, I said. I wanted to talk about anything else.

Hey, listen, I said. The activity fair is now, before

first period. I want to sign up for Model U.N. Do you wanna come?

Okay. Keeley finally looked at me. She smiled. God, she was beautiful. How had I never noticed that? Everything about her looked like she just shot out this glow, like without even trying she lit up.

I saw a flash of Keeley, years of Keeley, little kid Keeley. Taking off on her bike, leaning into my sister's ear whispering, leaning over a pile of construction paper, scissors, torn magazine pages—she was always making something. A collage, a poster; on her knees over a pile of paper and glue in our kitchen and then her eyes welling up when her parents would come to get her. I don't wanna go, she never wanted to go. And then she'd gone with them this summer. I hadn't thought about it. She'd gone this time. And now she was here, glowing.

The library was packed with tables hawking crap—school T-shirts and pens and last year's newspapers and promises of popularity if you signed up. Matthew Levitt was manning the M.U.N. table as usual. Damn poor Matthew Levitt. Matthew Levitt was a senior who had a ponytail and drove a vintage Chevy Nova and knew the guidance counselors by their first names and spoke quiet and fierce. I couldn't help but think that there was a place and time where the intensity and intellect of Matthew Levitt would be really exciting. But it wasn't here. And sometimes I couldn't help but be afraid that my slipping under the social radar actually put me closer to Matthew Levitt than I wanted to admit.

What's M.U.N.? Keeley whispered. She was right next to me, whispering against my neck. You're always going to M.U.N. meetings but I have no idea what that means.

It's, you know, like the United Nations but it's— like we all get assigned a country and debate the issues and...

I couldn't believe what an asshole I sounded like. It's lame, I said. Hey, I said to Matthew.

Hey man, said Matthew, looking at Keeley.

It's not lame. Keeley watched me sign my name. Matthew watched Keeley standing next to me. When I put the pen down Keeley picked it up.

I wanna try it, it sounds cool.

Matthew Levitt and I both stared at Keeley bent over signing her name, her blonde hair falling on the table.

Noelle

Keeley left for Oxford on the first day of summer vacation. The last night of school, we stayed up all night packing her suitcase. Her bedroom is round; it's in the turret of the house and has windows all the way around. It feels like you're sitting in the sky. She has long silver curtains that blow out from the window like clouds and brush along the floor, which is carpeted in Turkish rugs, one piled on top of the other. Her parents used to live in Turkey and the whole house is filled with rainbow-colored rugs, each one with its own story, and each one, they always tell us, made only of all-natural vegetable dyes.

Her paintings and collages paper the walls—photographs of us and swirling watercolors and magazine pages and pieced-together quotes. Whether it's the handmade rugs or the handmade wallpaper, it's like everything there was done by hand.

Keeley had one giant suitcase; it was bright green and deep enough to sit inside. We filled it with carefully chosen jeans (only the faded ones), and skirts of clingy fabrics and thin T-shirts and scarves, because overseas no one wore zip-up hoodies, they only wore scarves. She was going to spend the summer with her parents while they taught a special course about the guy who wrote *The Lord of the Rings* and spent all of his time writing and drinking with other famous people at a bar called the Eagle and Child. Keeley said her mom actually wanted to have the class at this bar. Meet there every day and read his stuff out loud. I didn't tell Keeley, because she seemed so mad about it all, but I kind of wanted to take that class. More and more when she talked about the stuff she was going to do, I realized that it was stuff I just couldn't do—I wouldn't get to do. Like go to England on vacation or look good in old boys' jeans.

Keeley was going to spend the whole summer in Oxford before our junior year and her whole life was going to change. I knew it. And mine was going to sit in place.

Should I bring this? Keeley held up her favorite shirt. It was a long-sleeved gray baseball shirt and the ends of the sleeves were worn thin. When I looked up at her face, there were tears spilling out of her eyes.

What's wrong? I jumped up to hug her.

I just don't wanna go, she said. I just wanna stay here with you. I just wanna stay in this room. She waved around her. Keeley never liked being away from home. Even when she was at our house, we never could have sleepovers. Sometimes she'd creep up the hill at three in the morning. It wasn't that she wanted to be there when her parents woke up. It wasn't that she wanted to be around them. There was just something for her about the safety of her turret. About the safety of places where she could be alone.

Listen, I told her then. It's going to be great. You're going to England. There are going to be so many beautiful older guys with that great accent. You'll have your own room with a view of... what's that river called?

Keeley laughed.

The Cherwell, she said. She always knew.

She started to fold her sweater again absently.

You'll be, like, Miss I've-seen-the-world, I told her. It was my job to make her feel safe with things. To make her feel better. It was her job to make me feel better. That was how it was.

God I'm gonna miss you, she said. Promise we'll talk every day?

Every day. Maybe two times a day?

She looked at me. She bit her lip and wiped at her tears with the back of her hand.

Noelle, she said, I'm afraid we're not going to talk every day. I don't know why, but I'm afraid.

I remember when she said that. I remember it clearly. Because it was in that moment when I realized that, since we were five years old, I'd never not seen Keeley for more than a few days at a time. I'd never had to talk to her in any way but right in front of me. What was this going to mean? I was scared to ask her. It was the first time I was ever scared to ask her anything.

When she came back, when school started, when the summer started to fall away and the leaves were turning gold and then brittle brown, while all of this was happening, I couldn't get close to Keeley. It was like I couldn't find her.

And I was distracted.

*   *   *

The first Friday after school started, Jessica called me. I hadn't seen Parker since the night at her brother's loft, but I thought about him for at least part of every minute of every day.

Jessica called and said Parker had told her brother to call me and Jessica and invite us to some party in the city.

Just wear something sexy, Jessica told me.

I had no idea what that was. I stared at my closet. I tried to think what she would wear. Finally, I wore jeans and a black T-shirt. The T-shirt was old. It was Lace's and faded thin and sort of sheer-looking in the right light.

When we arrived at the house, it was spilling people onto the crooked front porch and the dead, brown lawn. It wasn't even Parker's house. Jessica thought maybe it was someone he worked with. There were people everywhere—people in thick-soled boots and white tank tops and stringy black hair and dirty jeans and tattoos. There was smoke sitting in the hallways and music from rooms, slow and mourning from one doorway and fast and sad from another door. Even Jessica seemed a little bit nervous. We finally found Parker and her brother sitting in a bedroom. There was a twin bed and some pillows on the floor, and Parker was sitting next to a girl who was wearing a shirt with a belt over it and high red boots, and her legs were white and long and looked like bones. I stared at her.

Hey, he said. He got up and hugged Jessica and then me. But then he gestured to me.

Sit down.

I did. Jessica sat next to her brother's friend Tommy on the bed.

So. Parker looked at me. You made it.
Yeah, I said.

Everyone was quiet for a long time.

Parker, the girl with red boots said.

He turned to look at her. Then he looked down at his hand.

Oh, you want some? he said to me.
Um. Okay.

The girl rolled her eyes.

I took the joint from his fingers, touching the coarse skin of his thumb. I took a hit and held it in, my throat burned but I held the cough deep in my chest. I took another hit. My eyes watered. I pretended I was sneezing, coughing into my hand. I handed the joint back to Parker.

We were alone in the room and the lights seemed to be swimming at the ceiling above a curtain of smoke. I didn't know where everyone had gone. Parker was watching me smoke the cigarette he'd just given me. I ashed it toward a green bottle, missing and scattering ashes on the carpet. His eyes on me felt like pins and needles. I wanted to touch him.

Do you go to school? I asked instead.

He shook his head.

No. I graduated two years ago.
College?

He laughed.

> I graduated high school.
> Oh.
> I cook in a restaurant.

This sounded glamorous to me, the idea of him cooking. I thought of the fire tattoo on his hand.

> You like it?
> Oh, man. Suddenly his eyes shifted. I started washing dishes when I was a kid. But I loved being in the kitchen. People don't realize it's art, making good food. It's seriously art. I'm gonna have my own place one day ... it's not gonna be this shit mango salsa on everything. It's gonna be food no one has ever even had before ... His voice trailed off. He stared at a spot on the wall over my head. I watched him. It was quiet.
> I've been reading this book, he finally said.
> Yeah?
> Yeah. I mean, it says "man is something that shall be overcome." It basically says ... I mean, the thing is, we all try to find something we want to live for and succeed in but the real fucking bottom line is—he stops and looks at me. I like you, Noelle, he says.
> Thanks.

My head is spinning. Literally, like I am twisting around and around the room.

He takes the cigarette from my hand and drops it into the bottle. He leans into my ear and whispers.

And it's really hard for me to talk about food and work when all I want to do is kiss you.

Okay, I say.

I turn, my nose brushes against his cheek, and then he's kissing me and seriously my whole body is burning and out of breath all at once. I close my eyes but I can still see the light suspended at the ceiling and I'm sinking into the cushions and floating underneath him at the same time.

Nadio

My sister was busy doing something none of us knew about. In the first few weeks of school it became clear she had something else going on. I was barely alone with Keeley once in those first weeks but it was like Noelle started moving away from us even before we started moving together.

It really had been easy to be the three of us. Keeley and Noelle were pretty much attached. Their voices came out in unison—a sentence started with one of them and finished with the other. They never considered a move without each other. And Keeley understood about Noelle and me. People get freaked out by the twin thing, or they get really curious, but Noelle and I just always preferred to be near each other without saying much. I was never one for saying much. And she knew what I was thinking anyway. But even before Keeley left for Oxford, I noticed Noelle pulling back. I'm not sure she even noticed it, but I did.

She doesn't even care about the things she gets, she said about Keeley after helping her pack. It's like she gets to travel all over the world and she just, she resents it. Noelle's face was tight when she said this. She has no idea about how lucky she is, she said and walked away and I heard her door slam. I doubt she even realized I was a part of her monologue. I felt her jealousy even through the walls.

That jealousy got fierce after school started. It was quiet, too.

On Friday night, Keeley knocked on the screen door. I was sitting at the kitchen table with HDT. Lace was in her room. Noelle was somewhere.

Hi, Keeley said through the screen.

I looked up. I actually thought about what I was wearing and wished I hadn't changed into sweatpants after school.

Hey, I said.
Can I come in?
Yeah, of course. I stood up. Noelle's not here.
Oh.
Do you want some tea?

She giggled. I felt like an asshole again.

Do you wanna go for a walk? she asked.
Yeah. I practically tossed the book across the room.
Lemme just run up and get some shoes...

I took the stairs two at a time. I pulled on jeans and
shoved my feet into sneakers.

I'm going for a walk, I called to Lace. I heard a
murmured response. The thing about Lace, she certainly
never imposed strict rules. Be safe, she said. Call me if
you're sleeping out, she said. Never, ever, turn your cell
phone off. She wanted us to be safe, to tell her anything,
and she wanted to be able to reach us. Period.

Keeley was standing on the porch, her back to me. I
walked up behind her. Without even looking she reached
her hand back and waved it around until she held mine.

Keeley Shipley was holding my hand.

We started walking. Finally she looked over at me.

You know, you're the only person I want to be around since I came back.

I just kept staring at her. Was she always this beautiful? Did I never notice?

Nadio. It's weird, right?

I blinked my eyes back into focus. I squeezed her hand. I stopped walking.

Yeah, I said. It's weird. I think about you pretty much all the time.

I brought my hands up to the curve of her jaw. I leaned in and kissed her. I felt her hands in the belt loops of my jeans, pulling me closer. We kissed for a minute, three hours, I don't know. Keeley finally pulled back, reaching up and pushing my hair off of my forehead.

God, I wish we'd figured this out years ago. She laughed, but her eyes were jumpy. Her laugh sounded like she was pushing it out of her.

Me too, I said.

Let's sit. Keeley pointed. We had walked up the

driveway alongside the orchard and we were near her house. There were a few Adirondack chairs sitting around an old fire pit. I sat down. Keeley climbed onto my lap, tossing her legs over the arm of the chair.

Let's talk about something that's not Noelle, that's not how weird this is, she said.

Okay, but—

I put my hand on the small of her back. It was hard for me to breathe, her sitting like this, her arm around my neck.

I might not be able to concentrate, I said.

She laughed again. That laugh was nervous and confident all at once—giggling and all-knowing.

Nadio, did you ever have a girlfriend?

I thought about last spring, volunteering at the St. Francis soup kitchen. Molly from the college. From the first day she started working there she'd put her hand on my arm every time she said anything and laugh really close to my neck. Then she started pulling me into the dry goods supply closet and tugging my jeans down. Molly wore tight

T-shirts and miniskirts and she was very sure of everything.

I silently thanked Molly for the supply-closet hours.

No, I said. Not really.

I didn't need to tell Keeley about Molly. She wasn't really my girlfriend. Besides, this summer she'd transferred to somewhere out west. On her last day, as she was pulling her T-shirt back on over her head, she smoothed it over her stomach and rested her hand on my arm. Well, Nadio, she said. This has been awesome. She giggled. I hope you find a real sweet girlfriend and I know you'll make her happy.

And that was that.

Why not? Keeley asked.
I don't know, I said. I guess no one ever before now, I never thought anyone was really—
Worth it? Keeley asked.
I guess. What about you?

Keeley shivered.

You know, she said, the truth is, I don't think anyone ever noticed me.

What about this summer? I asked. I knew that, now, Keeley couldn't go anywhere unnoticed. Did you meet anyone?

Keeley's fingertips stopped scratching the back of my neck. I felt them rest, tense and cold, at my hairline.

You know what Nadio? I'm gonna be honest. I don't wanna talk about this summer.

The air felt heavy. We sat in silence. Keeley's whole body was like a knot.

Let's talk about good old Henry David Thoreau. I saw what you were reading, she finally said.

Yeah?

Love him.

You do?

Sure, Keeley said. My parents used to read the Transcendentalists out loud to me. You know, they've always been really good at understanding kids. Her voice was dry and heavy when she said this—somewhere between sarcastic and truth.

I can see why you were always at our house, I said.

She leaned down and kissed me again.

It's my dad's book, I said when we pulled apart. I don't know why I told her that.

Keeley stared at me.

Neither one of you has ever even said the word dad in my presence.

Yeah, I said. It was Dario's book.

Noelle

It's possible I could drop out of school, I thought. Not that it was actually something I'd do. But I was almost sixteen, and I can't be here, I thought. It was like my body was physically resistant to the curve of the plastic Chem-class chair. My mind was certainly resistant to Mr. Donohoe's droning lectures, which came to me through a curtain of static. I looked around. Two people were sleeping. Mark Hoolihan and Louis Dayton were doing a crossword puzzle. Mr. Donohoe was drawing something on the board, gesturing at us.

I'll never make it.

When he turned his back to face the board again, I

picked up my bag and slid out of the classroom into the empty hallway.

Was he going to come after me?

Was he going to notice?

I leaned on a locker, closed my eyes. My head felt like it was swimming. The door to the chemistry room stayed closed.

Once, I used to be good at school. Of course I was nothing like my brother—Nadio is so smart it's scary. He asked questions the teachers never knew how to answer. It's like his mind works at a level that is one step above everyone else. But I used to be pretty good. I used to like being there. I wanted something out of all of it. I asked questions. Explain it to me, I don't get it.

But that day, all I could think about were Parker's cold-water eyes, his hand against any part of me—the back of my neck, my thigh...

Noelle?

It was Keeley.

Oh. Hey.

What are you doing? she asked.

I just—I nodded behind me. I couldn't handle Chem class.

I waited. I waited for her to tell me I had to get back, I'd get in trouble.

I have study hall, she said. But that library is claustrophobic. She half smiled. She looked nervous.

You wanna go—

We can sit by the track, I said. No one ever goes back there.

We started to walk down the empty hallway. I felt like I could grab hold of the silence between us. I realized Keeley didn't even know about Parker.

I didn't know a thing about her summer. It made me want to keep Parker a secret. Just because Keeley left town didn't mean she could be the only one with secrets.

Nole, she said. We pushed through the double doors onto the back fields.

Yeah?

I had the feeling she was going to say something big. One of us had to say it. What happened to us? Where

are we going? It was like this silence between us was frozen and we were both feeling our way around it. How
is it that two people can need each other so absolutely
and then, in moments, not even know how to be next
to each other and just be quiet? I snuck a look at Keeley.
She was staring toward the track but her eyes were glass,
like inside she was staring at something completely
other. Her hair covered half of her face, a shiny, perfect gold curtain. She was wearing her boots again, and
some weird long sweater over thick tights. On top of it
all was an old faded navy-blue hoodie, and she had her
fists clenched up inside the sleeves.

Is that my brother's sweatshirt?

Her face froze. Then she broke into weird high breathy
laughter.

I was cold in English. It looks ridiculous, doesn't it?
Yeah, I said. I tried to laugh with her. It does look
ridiculous. But I couldn't, quite.

Keeley stopped and looked at me now, her eyes serious.

Seriously, Noelle. Do you ever feel—

Just then Jessica Marino crashed through the double doors behind us.

Noelle! She was breathless. I just ditched Pre-Calc. I swear that woman is going to kill me. Let's get outta here. I gotta smoke a joint and eat a cheeseburger. I'm having such a craving.

She pulled on my arm. It was quite possible she didn't even see Keeley.

I'm sorry, I said to Keeley. I was talking to her over my shoulder. Jessica was already pulling me away.

Keeley shrugged. She'd pulled her sleeves up in front of her mouth.

We'll hang out, I said.

Keeley stood there. She never said a word.

Nadio

When she walked into the room, I could tell Keeley had been crying. Classroom lights are unforgiving. Her eyes were swollen. She had her sleeves pulled over her fists, and she kept bringing them up to rub her eyes. She was late and Matthew Levitt was talking about the Human Rights committee and they were slacking and needed their resolutions by today to submit—

He was still talking as I stood up, walked to the back of the room, and edged Keeley back out into the hallway.

What happened? I asked her.

She was staring at her toes. She was silent for a while.

She is so mad at me, she said.
Noelle?

She looked up. She stared at me like I was suddenly unrecognizable, her eyes blank and furious at once.

It's like, it's not even about you and me. Do you think she even knows? And it's not even like she's mean. She's just outright cold, like we were never even inseparable friends for our whole lives. It's like she's mad at me for everything that's wrong in the world. It's like she's mad at me for breathing. And there's nothing I can even say. I'm trying so hard to keep our friendship. What happened to it? Where is she all the time?

Keeley kept talking and her voice sounded like gasping. I knew none of her questions wanted answers.

I felt myself sighing. I knew my sister. I didn't have to know what had happened. Probably nothing happened. Probably Noelle just froze Keeley out. Made her feel like she was barely there.

What decides the kind of people we are? Really. Noelle and I were born at the exact same time. Almost. One mother. No father. One house. Everything about the way we grew up was exactly the same. What made us so different? Even before we started school—before we watched other kids from other families and learned how to "be"—even then Noelle could turn rock hard when she was upset. I'd run around trying to make her or Lace feel better and tell jokes or find cookies or whatever, and Noelle would set her lips in this thin hard line and narrow her eyes and that was that. Until she was ready to stop being mad.

Look, I said. I put my hand on Keeley's arm.

She's so mean to me, Keeley said. She took a deep breath.

Keeley. I said her name and then I didn't want to keep talking. But she was staring at me, waiting. You can do things, have things... I stopped. I shouldn't go on. Keeley was staring at me.

Look, I said again. We live in your gatehouse, Keeley. Gatehouses used to be for servants. I know it's not that way now, but look—Noelle worked at an ice cream stand while you went to Oxford...

Keeley pulled her arm away.

Oh fuck, she said.
I don't mean...
Jesus. She backed up.

Keeley, I'm not saying I feel this way. I'm just saying, I'm just trying to say what my sister is. I mean, I think Noelle is jealous. That makes people mean. I don't know what's going on with her, but…

I have to go, Keeley said, turning.

Look, she's mad at me too, I said. But Keeley was running down the hall. She pulled the hood of my sweatshirt up over her head as she pushed out through the front door of the school.

I don't go back into the room. I slide my back down the wall and sit on the floor of the empty hallway.

Fuck, I answer Keeley.

Dear Dario;
How could she know? When do we start to feel the differences between us? When do we stop being kids who just want each other's company and start being complicated by all these other things? When do we wake up and have to be aware of how much money one of us has? Or who is going to feel like running away to escape this life? How could any of us know that one of these days it was going to be impossible to just be perfectly three together? Three never works.

But you wouldn't know any of this. Only one worked for you.

Noelle

I started going to Parker's house after school. I didn't want to be anywhere else. Jessica would drive me into the city, or I could catch a bus in front of the post office. But the bus felt weird—no one I knew took the bus and if anyone saw me standing there, waiting, I'd have to explain where I was going. I couldn't explain it—it was a secret journey made all the better because only I knew about it.

Nadio and I would be getting our licenses soon, but for now I needed a ride. I snuck on the bus, I rode my bike.

From the main road, I had to cut through a parking lot, which was always empty and I could enter the apartment through the garage downstairs, which was always open. The garage was called Sammy's, and the only cars in there looked like they'd been crushed by a huge truck or a wrecking ball. There were no small repairs at Sammy's.

Sammy was nice to me. He waved and let me up the back staircase, so I didn't have to climb the rickety metal staircase winding up the side of the building that was Parker's main entrance. Sometimes he gave me mail or even a cup of coffee to bring up to Parker. He always told me to be careful, but he didn't mean it like there was anything dangerous. He seemed to mean it the way a dad would, like reminding me to just look after myself.

Because he lived above a garage, Parker's apartment always smelled a little bit like burning rubber and gasoline. There was something about it that was toxic and addictive. I loved that smell.

Sometimes Parker would be sleeping on his couch. Sometimes he would be reading and smoking a cigarette on his bed. Sometimes he wouldn't be there at all and I'd just wait for him. The thing about him: he made me feel like I could be noticed. Like someone noticed me. And that I was worth it. No one had ever made me feel that way before.

And sometimes he made me feel invisible.

After I left Keeley standing by the back field, after Jessica and I smoked a joint and she ate a cheeseburger with one hand and held a cigarette in the other and drove at the same time, after that I asked her to bring me to Parker's.

Jesus, I hope you're sleeping with him by now.

She licked her finger and crumpled the empty foil cheeseburger wrapper into a tiny ball.

No, I said.

I wasn't. Despite his best efforts.

Okay, said Jessica. She pulled the car over and turned to look at me, dropping cigarette ash onto her lap as she did.

Parker seems to like you, Noelle, but baby, listen, you're not going to hang on to him this way. Just get it over with! After the first few times you'll start to have fun. Believe me.

I believed her. Sort of. How could I explain how terrified I was? How could I tell Jessica Marino how I was afraid

I'd do everything wrong, how most of all I wanted Parker to be there, not just with anyone, but I wanted him to want to be there with me.

Sometimes when I was with him I felt like I could be just about anyone who was almost naked.

But I couldn't tell Jessica this.

You're so right, I said. Listen, I'm gonna walk from here. I got out of the car and leaned in. Thanks, I said.

Good luck, baby, she called after me.

I didn't feel any better. I could see Keeley standing alone on the field. I could see Jessica shaking her head as I walked away. I could see Parker, the crescents of his hip bones just above the waist of his jeans, the wiry muscles in his arms moving slowly under the inked designs as he pushed my jacket back off my shoulders and slipped the buttons of my shirt open.

Sammy handed me two cups of coffee as I came in.

Good to see you, sweetie, he said.

When I opened the door to Parker's apartment, he was

sitting at the table, leaning over a book with his head in one hand, a cigarette burning in the other.

Hey, he said, looking up.

He pushed his chair back from the table. The book fell closed. I glanced toward the cover, trying to look like I wasn't looking. A painting, thin strokes, the title in fragile white letters: *The Birth of Tragedy*.

He looked at my eyes on the cover of the book. I felt him and I looked up. He seemed to smile at me.

Hi. I put the coffee down on the table and let my bag slip off my shoulder.

He took a drag on his cigarette and stubbed it out. He nodded at the book.

Read it? he asked.
No, I said.
Com'ere.

I walked over to him. My heart was racing all the way into my throat. He pulled me into him so his cheek was against my stomach. Then he pushed my shirt up and kissed my stomach. I felt all at once like I never wanted to be anywhere else other than that gasoline-smelling apartment, and like I wanted to throw up.

Let's do something, I said, putting my hand on top of his head, trying to push it back as gently as I could.

He tucked his finger into the waist of my jeans, not looking up.

Mm-hmm.
Like, go somewhere. I took his hand and held it.

He finally looked up.

Where d'you wanna go?

I suddenly wished I hadn't said anything. I felt my face flush.

I don't know. We always—we're just here. We could go, like, eat something.
Eat something? He smiled slowly.

What I wanted to say was, we never talk about anything. We just kiss. Then you take my pants off. Then my throat closes and my heart rushes and I push you away and you say what's wrong and I say I don't know. What I wanted to say was, I want to feel like you want to be with me as a real live couple. Then I'll be ready to sleep with you.

Instead I said, Never mind. I don't know.

And he pulled me down onto his lap.

Wait, I wanted to say. Wait. I could feel him kissing my neck but it wasn't my neck now, it was my neck the first time he kissed me, before anyone (who wasn't related to me) had ever kissed any part of me, neck or otherwise.

And I couldn't say anything. The ridges of his fingers felt coarse along my stomach. I shivered. I didn't want to say anything.

Wait, I said.

He sighed.

Nadio

I couldn't concentrate.

Last year it was easy. Run, study, ace tests, work at the food pantry, Model U.N. I had a routine. It was every minute. I knew the things I wanted to do. This year I quit the food pantry. I actually really liked being there, Molly or no Molly—there was something therapeutic about stacking can after can of green beans, box after box of Stove Top, and something comforting about packing boxes for distribution ... one of everything, knowing that meals that would come out of that box would be so much more important than any meal I ever ate.

But I just couldn't do it this year. If I wasn't at school, I wanted to be with Keeley.

After the night she came to my kitchen door it was like we just became a couple. Keeley didn't want to talk about it, which worked for me. But everything we did, the way we looked for each other, the way I decided everything I would do with her in mind, that must be what being a couple is like. We were just a couple who couldn't quite tell the public truth.

I was at lunch, returning my tray to the dish window, when Keeley grabbed my arm.

Come on, she whispered.

And I realized in the buzzing crowd and anonymous noise of high school lunch time, we could sneak out in the middle of hundreds of people.

Without talking, Keeley pulled my hand down the nearly empty hallway, up the cold concrete stairwell to the second floor and, turning a corner, she pushed open the door of the boys' handicapped bathroom. White-gray tile floors, a crooked urinal, a toilet. A finger-print-streaked silver bar ran the length of the room to the sink that Keeley was leaning up against. I could see myself in the mirror above her head, her blonde hair at my chin. My eyes surprised me—to see myself there surprised me. I looked exactly like me but something in my eyes looked stretched, looked tense, looked almost desperate.

I moved toward Keeley.

Hi, she said.

I didn't say anything. I kissed her. I put my hands at the base of her neck to pull her closer to me. Her mouth was warm and slow. She slid her hands up my back. Everything about her felt slow and soft. I could feel the tumbling beat of her heart through my shirt. Her tongue pressed against mine and then back. I tried to pull her closer. I brought my hand down her neck, her side; and under her T-shirt the skin of her stomach was hot. Her back folded against the sink. Then she stopped. Her whole body stopped.

Wait, she said.

I felt like I'd been running too fast to stop myself, like I'd tumbled forward head first.

She pushed against my chest.

Just hang on, she said. She rubbed her hand over her eyes, pushed her hair back.

Okay, I said. I was picking myself up, breathing like the sprint was over. I stood with a foot between us.

Are you okay, I asked, counting my breaths, trying to slow them.

Yeah, she said. She lifted her head and looked at me. She tried to smile. Sometimes it's just really fast.

But you, I wanted to say, you pulled me up here. I didn't say anything. I watched her. Sometimes I didn't get it— I didn't get her. She was holding on to something.

Yeah, I said to her. It is. It's okay.

Her smiled was relieved now.

I mean, she said, I love kissing you. I don't want you to think I don't.

But I didn't want to talk about this. I didn't want us to say why or why not or explain through all of it.

Hey, I said. We still have some time before next period. Want an iced tea or something?

Okay.

Keeley moved forward. She leaned up and kissed my cheek.

You're kind of amazing, she said. She looked almost sad. Let me walk out first. I'll meet you outside the cafeteria in five minutes.

Okay, I said. I'll be right behind you.

It was like this a lot with me and Keeley. We found all of these hiding places—her attic, groves in the orchard, even that second floor handicapped boys' bathroom. We had to find hiding places because neither one of us was ready to tell Noelle. And the truth was, what would we tell Noelle anyway?

Sometimes Keeley and I couldn't get enough and she leaned into me when I slid my hand up her stomach and under her bra, and she tried to pull me closer to her and even sometimes she bit at the skin on my neck under my left ear. But then sometimes she froze and stopped and turned off and pushed me away.

There was no way of knowing how it would go when we were together. And those times when she pushed me away, she looked so sad that I couldn't do a thing. That I swallowed that sharp ball of frustration and sometimes even anger. I thought I knew where the anger was coming from, though, and it wasn't just her.

*   *   *

I finished *Walden*, I told Lace after dinner one night. I was helping her do the dishes. Noelle had just left, claiming she was going to Jessica's to study. I could see that her backpack was empty as she walked out the door. Lace shook her head.

Be careful, she called out. But Noelle didn't look back.

What did you think? Lace asked.
Well...

Dario, he... your dad. He said he loved America when he read that book. He said, for him, he didn't even know what solitude felt like. He said Italians smother each other. The only way you get to know anything about yourself or the world you live in is through the eyes of your family.

She was looking down while she talked, scrubbing one spot on the plate in her hands over and over.

Ironic, huh? She smiled at me.

Mom? Why don't we ever talk about him?

She stopped washing. Noelle and I hardly ever called her Mom. Ever since we could talk, we'd reveled in the sound of her name.

Do you want to?

Kind of.

She wiped her hands on a dish towel and sat down at the kitchen table. I sat across from her.

I know, I said, because she seemed nervous. I know you were seventeen. I know you were traveling in Italy. I know that for a whole year you were in love and then, when you were pregnant, he disappeared. I know this part, Mom, and I hate him for this part. But I feel like I need to know who he was.

She nodded.

Shit, she said.

I started to feel guilty. I couldn't help but think how she and my dad were just about the same age I am. Noelle is. Keeley is.

I was so independent, Lace said. I graduated high school early, I'd lost my parents, I knew what I wanted. I was never afraid of traveling alone . . .

I knew all of this but I let her talk. I felt like she was warming up. My whole body felt tight, like I was waiting for something to break open.

He was just beautiful, she said. He was exactly what I needed, right then.

Lace reached across the table. She put her hand over mine. She was staring over my head.

Nadio, it was like . . . it was like when I met your dad everything opened. He just pulled me everywhere. He spoke the language and suddenly everything was possible. People seemed to know him everywhere. They didn't, of course, but he was just so fucking charming.

Her hand gripped mine on the table.

There's so much about him. He knew—he just knew. He knew where to dig for truffles. He knew the back roads. He knew about the widow in every village who had rooms and would cook us breakfast and dinner. He read books in three different languages. He knew all about growing and harvesting grapes and cooking the most amazing meal with four ingredients. He made me feel like there was no one else in the world.

She stopped. Her eyes slid back into focus. She looked at me.

That was really what it was—being the only two people in the world. You'll feel it one day and you'll know what I mean. It's different for women, though, I have to say, Boo. I don't think you need to feel needed as much as we girls do. Her grip loosened. Am I wrong?

I don't know, I said. I'd never thought about it that way.

She squeezed my hand again. This time it wasn't desperate. It was comfort.

Don't hate him.

I stood up, pulling my hand away carefully. I leaned down and kissed her head.

Thanks, Lace.

Her eyes were gone again.

Okay, she whispered.

Noelle

Parker's back was to me. My tank top was twisted high around my stomach.

I felt naked.

I couldn't help it. Sometimes I thought about Lace and our dad. I thought about how they were so close to my age. I thought about how they were on the other side of the world and there was no one else but them. That's what she once said it felt like. It was weird to think about them while I was here. But some part of my mind just fell to them.

There was no one in the world but Parker and me. I imagined it for just a second. It was just the two of us and nothing else was on the other side of the bedroom door.

But the apartment was freezing. The sheet was wrapped around him. I reached out to pull it toward me. I stopped. It was wrapped around his waist and through his legs. He was sleeping. I couldn't wake him.

Jesus, Noelle, what's the problem? he'd said.
I just feel ... I could never finish my sentences with him.

He was sitting up. His eyes looked raw. He pushed his hair back, rubbed his hand across his face. He was somewhere between exhausted and angry.

We can start and stop this only so many times, you know. You need to tell me what you want. That's how this goes.

I wanted to disappear. Even my name seeped out of his lips covered in frustration. Maybe even exhaustion.

I don't know what I want, I'd said.

He shook his head.

You seemed to two minutes ago.

Two minutes ago it had been different. But I couldn't say any of this out loud to him. I wanted to so badly. I wanted to explain that even his breath on my neck, the calluses on his fingers against my skin, the way he scooped my hair off my shoulder, that all of it was exactly what I wanted, but I was scared. Two minutes ago I was almost ready to go all the way through with it, and then he pressed his fingertips into the undersides of my wrists and I couldn't move.

Stop, I'd said.

I could feel every muscle in his body like a rubber band. He pushed himself off of me and sat up, his back to me.

Christ, he'd said.

I just want to know what you're thinking, I whispered.

He was quiet.

To be honest, I'm not thinking much of anything right now.

That was it. That was everything I knew and everything I didn't want to hear. It was every reason I stopped him even when I didn't want to.

Think about me, think about me, a voice inside my head pleaded.

But he was asleep.

Right then I did want to be somewhere else. I sat up slowly. It was dark outside. After dinner maybe. In the light from the streetlamps I reached around me: sweater, jeans, one sock, another sock. As I got dressed, buttoned my coat, picked up my bag, he never moved.

I took the bus home and when it left me in front of the post office, the whole town was quiet. A fat yellow square of light rested on the street in front of the Coyote Café. It had to be instinct that pulled me down the street to peek in the front window.

There she was.

For the past year or two, Keeley would sometimes come down to the Coyote and sit at the counter to do her homework. Sometimes she ate a bowl of chili or had two cups of hot chocolate, or sometimes she just asked for tap water and she read. No one ever minded her being there. Everyone knew who her parents were, and probably knew they were rarely home between night-time lectures and committees and student conferences. All of the things, Keeley used to say, that came before her.

Before she left for Oxford, if she wasn't at our house and I couldn't find her at home I could walk into town and find Keeley at the Coyote.

She was sitting there, her head bent over textbook pages that shimmered in the café light. Suddenly I wanted nothing else but to sit down next to her and have a coffee with hot milk and tell her how Parker turned his back and fell asleep. I wanted her to be the only one who knew what I meant when I talked about the inked slope of his back like a graffitied wall and being afraid to pull the sheet over me.

Hey. I slid onto the stool next to her. The café was empty except for a couple leaning in over their dinner in the back corner.

Keeley looked up, her eyes wide.

Hi. She smiled.

I looked down at the margin of her notebook. She was doodling. A sweeping wave down the college-ruled lines. I thought of the pictures above my bed. Keeley and I at ten, eleven, fourteen, gap-toothed and smiling, holding on to each other. For my birthday last year she'd arranged these years of photos on posterboard, painting borders around each in her swirling colored hand, like the photographs themselves were painted on. Almost ten years of us smiling for Keeley's camera—it was always Keeley's camera, our parents never took the pictures. And all of the pictures the same: Keeley on the right as she held her arm above us to take the picture, me leaning in to fit in the frame.

Hey, Keeley said again. Then she leaned over and hugged me and my eyes felt hot. I sucked the tears back to the pit of my stomach.

Trig? I nodded at her textbook.

What? Oh yeah. Noelle, what's going on? Where were you?

She put her hand over mine on the countertop.

Nowhere, just … listen. I'm sorry I left you before.

It's okay, she lied.

I just had to—I stopped. I didn't even have the strength for another lie. I sort of met this guy.

Tell me! I knew it was something. She squeezed

my hand and then moved hers away. In that moment, though, the space between us felt okay.

I don't know, Kee. He's so hot, he's like—there's something about him I can't even tell you. His eyes, they're like this crazy gray-blue. And he has his own apartment. He's nineteen and he cooks, but it's like— cooking isn't like his job, it's like his complete passion. Every piece of clothing he owns is like paper thin and beat down and he has this square jaw and, oh my god, these tattoos—

I stopped. Keeley was watching me. She nodded.

His tattoos, they're like—I don't know. You know you get that feeling like your life isn't at all what it's supposed to be, like it's just sitting still, and then you see something that makes you realize, like, there's this whole other world. Kee. All over his skin there are these words and designs and pictures and all of it is like this whole world. And his skin—

Yeah, she whispered.

It's like—it's not even just about his skin but it's like this feeling I have that he knows—he just knows, you know. Like he knows what the world looks like and he knows how to cook things I've never even heard of and he knows what I want even before I do, and then I look at these designs, these tattoos, these, like, stories…

Like tattoos of what? Keeley leaned in, her chin on her hand. She looked so familiar, suddenly.

Well, there's like a serpent and a Celtic—

Don't tell me Chinese symbols! she squealed.

Well yeah, but he's not like that. He's not like the total poser you're thinking, Keeley. These symbols, every one of them, are like part of him.

A part of him? She looked doubtful.

At first, talking about him to Keeley had made him so real, had felt like what I always thought this should feel like. But now the look on her face felt all wrong. It wasn't like she didn't believe me, it was like she didn't get him. It was like after everything I'd said, she couldn't understand Parker. That didn't make any sense—that Keeley wouldn't understand me, wouldn't understand what I felt about Parker—it didn't make sense.

Suddenly, none of it felt right.

I stood up.

Anyway, I said. I was just coming back from his house and I saw you, so…

Are you leaving? She sat up straight.

Yeah, I have a lot of homework.

Noelle, wait. I wanna hear more. I just meant like, is he funny? Does he like the same music as you? Lemme buy you a coffee or something.

My hands felt cold. I felt the heat of the same tears flooding, rushing, I had to get out of there before all of my muscles broke.

I'll see you soon, Kee. I gotta go.

I practically ran out of the café. My face was still wet when I got home.

Nadio

The nights were dark earlier now. I had to wear two sweatshirts. But I was still mostly running at night. Pretty much every night now. And when I got out there, when I started going and ran and ran, I finally reached the place where my breath got clear again and the pain in my chest and my knees ran into the ground. At that point I thought I could pretty much run forever.

It cleared me. It was literally like removing a weight.

We were doing our homework in the kitchen after school when Keeley asked if she could run with me. I told her no. Her face right then seemed to freeze and shatter.

I'm sorry, I said. It's just my thing. It's my time, you know.

She nodded, her head moving in a curtain of hair, but she wouldn't look up at me.

I mean, maybe every once in a while we can. But at night I just need—

Nadio, I get it.

She lifted her head. There were tears on her frozen, shattered face.

I feel kinda lonely, that's all, she said. I feel like an idiot and I feel lonely.

Why? Even though I knew the answer, I asked.

Nadio. Kids don't really notice this stuff, do they? Whose family has more money? I just never got it. And then when I came home, you were sitting there in the dark and you were so safe. You were so home. I wanted to just be as close to you as possible. But now it's like everything I've done has been to push Noelle away. But I don't mean to—I never meant to.

I know, I said.

I watched her. She took deep breaths.

So what do I do? This is making me crazy. I've never doubted myself this way. I feel like she's making me this pathetic person, crying all the time. What do I do?

That I didn't know. I didn't want any of this at the expense of my sister. But it wasn't about Noelle and me. I thought that, then. I thought it was about Noelle and Keeley.

You get some ice cream, I said.

She giggled. She brushed the tears off her face with her long sleeves.

Ice cream?
Uh-huh.

We walked into town. I bought her a cone of cherry chocolate chip and she licked it slowly, leaning against the wall of the post office while the sun went down behind us. She smiled at me, licking her ice cream cone, offering me a taste, twisting her sleeve in her free hand.

Jesus, I'm glad I'm not in England anymore, she said.
Isn't there ice cream in England? I asked. But she just stared behind me.

When she was done, I left her at the Coyote Café to do homework and I came back up to the house to go for a run.

But I knew there was something she still wasn't saying. When I would fool around with Molly, she was like a maniac. Her hands moved so fast and her breath was so hot and it was like nothing could happen fast enough. Keeley was so different. She was slow and deliberate and she paused and took deep breaths.

Do you want me to stop? I'd still ask, every time she took that breath.

Sometimes she said no. Keep going.

Sometimes she said yes. Sometimes she said yeah, let's talk about something. She wanted to talk about when we were kids, she wanted me to remind her of stories that made her laugh. Before it all got grown-up and sex-complicated, she said.

But the thing is, we never had sex. She always said not now, not yet, when we got to that point.

*   *   *

I was near the end of my run, passing along the far ridge

of the orchard. You could see the tiny square lights of our house and then, up the hill, the wide white lights of Keeley's house tossing out across the lawn. My breaths were even now and my head felt light. I loved this feeling near the end, like I was floating. Needles ran up and down my legs and I stamped them out with each stride.

Dear Dario,

Here's a question from son to father. How long am I supposed to be okay with "not now"? I'm not sex-crazed or anything. Before Molly, even after Molly and before Keeley, I was fine without a girl. I'm not saying I can't live if I don't have sex with her. It's just, Keeley stands in this place where she's trying to swallow me up, and I want to let her, and then she stops and says never mind and breathes me back out and you know what? Sometimes I say it's okay, Keeley. Don't worry. But I feel seriously angry. Did I get that from you? That temper that flares inside me when I don't get it how I want it. I think it might be from you and so I do everything I can to push it down. What I want to know is how do I know if I love someone or if I'm just lusting after her? What I want to know is, what do I do if that person is my sister's best friend and I think my sister might be losing it even before she finds out about this. If I had a dad, this is what I'd ask him.

I end the letter in my head as I pull open the screen door. I mentally fold it in thirds and stuff it inside an envelope in the back of my brain, unmailed and undocumented. The light is on in the kitchen but the house is quiet. I kick my sneakers off and pour a glass of water. As I walk up the stairs, I switch off the kitchen light. It's almost completely black but I could walk this house blind.

There's no light coming from Noelle's room, but as I climb the last stair, I hear a sound. I stop. I hold still, the water in my glass sloshes onto my wrist. I know the sound. She's crying. I know the sound anywhere; it's almost like I can feel it behind my eyes. Deep sobs, gasps for breath, tears soaking. I freeze, while her breaths slow to deep gasps for air and the tears dry on her cheeks. I freeze while she cries and slows and stops, and then I walk into my room and shut the door so she never hears me.

Noelle

After the night I left his house and ran into Keeley, Parker and I didn't speak for almost two weeks. I wanted to call him. And for part of every single minute I wanted him to call.

But I knew I had to see if he would call me.

And my sixteenth birthday was coming up.

Nadio and I had always been the youngest in our class. Lace started us early because she had to work, because our birthdays fell on the cusp, because we could already read. But being younger than everyone else meant that sometimes big birthdays seemed to come and go and by the time we reached them, the excitement had faded. This year felt even more strange. The truth was, I didn't care about my birthday at all. Keeley and I had always talked about throwing a big party—even though her birthday was in May—we always said we'd have a party for the three of us and we'd all take turns driving somewhere, anywhere. But I hadn't practiced driving in months and I didn't much feel like taking the test, and Jessica said listen, I know this bar in the city and the bartender is friends with my brother— let's go there and have drinks for your birthday.

I knew she was trying to make me feel better that I hadn't heard from Parker.

I knew at a bar in the city, I might run into him, like we all just happened to be there.

When Lace asked us at dinner what we wanted to do for our birthdays, Nadio was quiet.

I don't feel like making a big deal, I said. I actually think I'm just going to sleep over at Jessica's.

Lace looked back and forth between us. My brother and I didn't look at each other. I know neither of us really wanted to have a family plan. But I also know how strange it felt not to want that. What would he do?

Yeah, Nadio said. I've never been much of a birthday person.

That part was true.

Lace shrugged.

Okay, she said. Okay.

But on the morning of our birthday she made us pancakes piled high with raspberries and butter and she gave each of us an iPod she couldn't afford and she drove us to school, which we almost never let her do anymore, and she watched us walk into the building. We could feel her watching our backs and so, without talking, we walked close together until we pushed through the front doors of the school, and then we turned in opposite directions.

Jessica and I got dressed at her house. I borrowed a black skirt and ankle boots that felt too high to walk in but made my legs look especially long. Jessica piled my hair on top of my head and told me to leave my gray T-shirt on.

So you don't look like you're trying too hard, you know, she said.

Jessica managed to never look like she was trying too

hard, but in secret, I always felt like I looked all wrong when she dressed me.

Her brother drove us to the bar downtown and introduced us to his friend, Graham, behind the bar. They shook hands and whispered to each other, then Jessica's brother told us he'd pick us up at 12:30 and don't be stupid.

Everything about the bar was dim and sort of slimy and we sat on round stools and a few middle-aged guys in flannel shirts played darts behind us.

It's her birthday, Jessica announced to Graham, leaning forward over the bar.

Well happy birthday, said Graham. Just don't tell me which birthday it is.

He put two beers in front of us and winked at Jessica as he walked down the bar to another customer. I looked around me. More middle-aged guys, some blonde girls and a few boys in pressed blue shirts.

Nobody looked like Parker.

Don't worry, Jessica said into my neck. My brother said he hangs out here a lot.

What! I turned to her. I felt sick.

And I got his number from your phone. I sent him a text and told him it was your birthday.

Jessica...

I could feel a round ball swelling inside my stomach, a sickness in my throat. She didn't understand. It was a secret. It was unspoken. Nobody could talk about me and Parker. It would ruin everything.

Oh cheer up, it's your birthday. Jessica knocked her plastic cup against mine. Let's play pool, she said.

Jessica was good at pool. I wasn't too bad. She had a table in her basement and sometimes we'd play there. I just wanted to be good enough so that none of the sweaty guys with heavy bellies wanted to lean over me and "help" my shot. I didn't need to worry, really; they were all leaning over Jessica, buying her beers and watching her bend slowly over the table. I hovered near the chalkboard at the wall, sipping my beer, holding my phone against my hip in my pocket. I wanted to be able to have fun without him. I wanted to have so much fun I'd forget about him altogether.

Jessica seemed to have forgotten I was there. She giggled

from inside a circle of flannel-shirt guys. She held her pool cue absently and accepted cold beers before her cup was empty. My beer was warm. It made my head hurt and my eyes feel heavy. I felt invisible. I pretended I was watching a game of darts. I pretended I was watching the hockey game on the TV. Graham refilled my beer.

On the house, birthday girl. He smiled. I knew he felt bad for me.

By the time Jessica's brother came, she was clinging to Graham behind the bar, giggling loudly and her shirt had lost two buttons. Her brother looked embarrassed as he peeled her off Graham.

I told you guys not to be stupid, he said to me.

I felt dizzy. I followed him out of the bar.

At her house, Jessica's brother carried her to her room and laid her down on the twin bed. I pulled her shoes and jeans off and folded her comforter over her.

It was over.

That was my birthday.

Jessica started to snore as I brushed my teeth and changed.

I set up my bed on the floor and pushed her lightly. Her breath caught and then she was quiet. I closed my eyes. I willed myself not to cry. He was busy. He was working. My head spinning, I started to count myself to sleep.

Hey, Jessica mumbled.

What? I lifted my head from the floor.

Your phone, she said, somewhere between sleep and awake.

It was there on the nightstand. Buzzing. Blinking. I reached for it and clicked it open. The little envelope danced under his name.

Read. I pressed *enter.*

happy birthday, beautiful girl

I clicked it shut. I held the phone in my fist, tucking my head back onto the pillow. My stomach danced.

Sixteen.

It was like that. It could be better than anything else.

Nadio

Birthdays were always bigger for my sister than they were for me. The celebrations we had were because of her. In the months before we turned sixteen, I think I knew that this would be the first birthday we didn't have together. I wasn't surprised when she said she'd go to Jessica's. And I was even relieved, because it meant I could spend my birthday with Keeley.

But part of it didn't feel right.

After school, Keeley pulled up alongside the bike rack where I was unlocking my bike.

Why don't you leave that thing there, she said, leaning out the window.

I looked up. She was smiling, her bare arm hanging over the car door, a green scarf wrapped around her neck.

How will I get home?

She laughed, and hit the car door with the palm of her hand.

Get in. I'll bring you home, birthday boy.

I slid into the passenger's seat and leaned in to kiss her. She put her hand up.

Not here, she said.

I leaned back, closed my eyes.

Listen, she said.

I could feel Keeley turning out of the school parking lot. I kept my eyes closed.

My parents are out, she went on. There is some big lecture tonight and then a dinner. So I have an idea.

An idea? I said, raising my eyebrows without opening my eyes.

Yea. Come over.

That's your idea?

Come over and we can order a pizza and watch a movie.

Hmm. I opened my eyes and watched her drive. The lowering sun caught on her hair.

Well? She glanced at me, smiled, then back to the road.

Not a bad idea, I said. Keeley slowed to a stop at a red light. I leaned over.

What about here? I asked.

What?

Can I kiss you here?

Keeley smiled, her eyes still on the red light. Then she turned and pressed her lips against mine. A car honked. Keeley pulled back.

No, she said. You gotta wait.

Keeley's house was dark and cool and smelled musty and like old leather. It was piled with carpets and books and the leather furniture was cracked. It always reminded me of someplace old.

In here, Keeley said.

I followed her into the kitchen, bordered in blue tiles,

the countertops and cabinets spilling magazines and yellowed newspapers. Keeley opened the fridge and pulled out a plate of cheese cut into fat leaning triangles. She emptied a package of crackers into the center of the plate and set it down on the kitchen table, a massive structure that looked like it had once belonged in a medieval hall and instead of chairs, there was a long bench on either side.

Have some, she said.

I put my bag down and sat on the bench, slicing a soft marbled cheese with the edge of a cracker. Keeley left the room. I heard her shuffling, then ordering a pizza, paper crumpling, then she came back. The cheese tasted creamy and moldy. I ate another cracker.

Keeley kneeled on the bench across from me. She leaned over the table and cut a piece of hard yellowish cheese. She ate it without a cracker.

Mmm, she said. I have a present for you.

She'd taken off her sweater and her arms were bare. I felt myself wanting to touch her skin. She seemed different in this house—more confident and in charge, somehow.

Okay. What is it?

She reached under the table and produced a square package wrapped in newspaper. She must have brought it with her from the other room. She handed it over the table to me.

Should I open it now? I balanced the package in one hand. I could feel it was a book, heavy and hard-cover but square.

Of course.

I pulled the paper back. The cover was dark brown, rough and faded leather. The binding was looped together with thin leather string and I could see the rough yellowed edges of paper peeking jagged from the edges of the book. Painted in black script, it read *On the occasion of his 16th birthday*. I touched the letters, they felt almost sticky. The paint was thick.

You made this? I looked up. Keeley was watching me. She smiled.

Well, she said, open it. I did more than stitch the

cover. She was grinning. I could feel the heat in my cheeks.

I folded the cover open. On the first page, in the same heavy black handwriting, she wrote *it started here*. The paper was rough and textured. The writing went along the top of the page in Keeley's looping, tilted script, here in thinner black paint. Below the writing, a photograph—the gatehouse, my house. It was sometime early in the fall; brown-red leaves dusted the steps and the yard.

Where did you get this? I still held the book in my hands but I was watching her. Her smile seemed different tonight. Like it was just there, not hiding anything.

I took it, silly. Just keep going.

I flipped the page. I realized why the delicate handmade paper felt so thick. On the back of each page was taped a section of map, cut to fit exactly. I looked closer at the map.

Remember, Keeley said, when you were little you were obsessed with Mt. Everest. You said when we climbed Snake Mountain, it was like you were training.

I looked up at her. The truth was, I hadn't remembered that. Not until just then.

Keep going, she whispered. Her cheeks were red. She leaned in closer, her body folded over the table.

The facing page was the entrance to the Snake Mountain trail, the crooked sign—it was late fall now, the trees bare of leaves. I flipped. The track at school, the outside of the soup kitchen, an M.U.N sign—she giggled when I stopped on that page.

I had to, she said.

On the backs of each page, a map. Some maps were of places I'd thought about, some of places Keeley imagined I'd love. Finally, the orchard, the crumbling stone wall, the map on the back of Concord, Massachusetts and as I peeked closer, a tiny blue circle. Walden Pond.

When did you—? Each page held a million moments I'd walked through and imagined. Keeley had documented a whole life in still pictures and carved up maps. The pages narrated a life I'd both remembered and forgotten, gave truth to places that had been blurry and uncertain.

Shhh, she said. Just keep going. There's a little more.

I turned another page. This map spread across two pages, this time drawn in Keeley's hand in red and orange, her tiny round script choosing the names of cities, drawings of a mask, boats, mountains, steaming coffee cups, all within the jagged-edged boot of Italy, and blue paint rose up from the page in points, surrounding the peninsula.

One day, Keeley said, we can go. When you're ready.

Her voice seemed far away. I could feel a photograph on the last page—the back cover—and I absently flipped to it. A blurred black-and-white photograph of Keeley standing in her kitchen, her hair tucked behind her ears, her hands holding forth a frosted cupcake.

I looked up as I closed the book, holding my hands on either side of the cover. Keeley was standing now, her back to the fridge, holding a frosted cupcake in the palm of her hand.

Happy Birthday, she said.
You made this, I said. She nodded.
The cupcake and the book, she said.

I've never gotten a present anything like this.

I wanted to make you something that was, you know, a testament. Sixteen is a big deal. I mean... Her voice trailed off.

Keeley, I said. Thank you. This is incredible.

She shifted, holding the cupcake.

Can I have it? I asked.

She came over to the table, holding the cupcake out to me. I took it and put it down. I leaned over the cheese plate and kissed her. She pushed the plate aside and climbed over the table. She sat on the table in front of me, her feet on either side of me. Leaning down she kissed my forehead and my ear. I put the book down on the bench next to me, still seeing its pages even as I put my hands on Keeley's ankles.

I just wanted to make sure you remembered everything, she whispered.

I do, I said. I pulled her off the table onto my lap. I would have told her I remembered just about anything but the truth was, I did see so much more suddenly. I did see us, not just in these familiar places but on the winding roads in the maps. The truth was I could picture it.

When the pizza arrived, Keeley sent me into the living room. When she came out with the pizza, she'd torn the top off the box and lit a candle stuck in the center of the melted cheese. We ate the pizza cross-legged on the floor and then we moved to the couch and put in a movie, but with Keeley lying on her side, between the couch and me, her bare arms over my stomach. I have no idea what the movie was.

It wasn't until I got home that I wondered how my sisters' birthday had been, that it occurred to me I hadn't just turned sixteen alone.

Noelle

Part of every minute felt like a dream. It was like I was walking around half awake with my head swimming in still water. I didn't want anything. I didn't want one bite of any meal or to sit in front of five minutes of TV or more than three sentences with my mom or Nadio or Keeley or Jessica. Everything I started to do felt too heavy to finish. He was all I could think about.

When I was around him he made me feel like he needed something about me. He made my skin stand up and everything inside me race.

When I wasn't around him, when he wasn't calling, everything stopped moving.

He did call, finally. I was standing near the front gates of school, waiting for Jessica to pick me up. I held my breath as I looked down at my phone.

Parker, the phone blinked up at me. The ringer was on silent. His name blinked in green block letters.

I clicked the phone open.

> What's up, he said. Like we'd just spoken.
> Nothing.
> So, are you gonna come over sometime?
> Do you want me to? I asked him.
> Yeah, he said. It sounded like he was yawning. Yeah, come over tonight. Come to this party with me.

When I hung up I could feel my heart in my throat. I went home and took a shower. I put on jeans and black boots and a tank top I usually slept in. It was trimmed in lace. The skin of my chest glared white through the trim. I pulled my hair up into a bun and drew black eyeliner around the rims of my eyes. Look at you all Cleopatra, he had said to me once. That was all I needed. I made sure everything I wore drew out the black in my hair and my eyes, drew out anything that made him compare me to a queen. I just wanted him to say it again.

He was in the shower when I got there. I sat down at the kitchen table and my hands and breaths were shaking. I tapped my feet to do something on purpose. I stared at the joint he'd left in the ashtray. I didn't feel bold enough to smoke it. I took deep breaths. Finally I leaned toward the table, listening closely to the rushing sound of water, the hissing of pipes from the bathroom. I snuck two quick hits. I placed the joint carefully at just the angle he'd left it, fanning at the smoke that sat in the air. I breathed in and out. By the time he came out, his jeans hanging just below his hipbones, pulling a T-shirt over his head, I felt high and sleepy.

I shivered at the sight of him.

Hey, you, he said.

He leaned over to kiss me, slipping his hand inside my shirt.

I like this shirt, he said.
I missed you, I whispered. I didn't mean to say it out loud.
Yeah? He pulled me out of the chair.
Let's go, he said.
Really?

You wanna go places. Let's go to this party.

He held my hand as we walked down the stairs and the whole way to the party, but it was still like I wasn't even there. His hand felt cold and he barely talked the whole way. The party was at the same house where he first kissed me, only there were way less people there. Right away when we walked in he looked around, nervous. He kissed the top of my head.

I'll be around, okay? I'll find you.

I felt paralyzed. I stood alone in the hallway for a minute. I didn't belong here. Should I leave? Why did he even bring me? My mouth felt dry and I wanted to sit down. I walked down the hallway, past a couple whispering in a doorway. They didn't even look at me. See, I thought. They don't care. No one even notices I'm here.

I didn't know if that made me feel better or worse.

I was standing in the kitchen.

The skeleton girl with red boots was standing at the sink. She was holding an empty glass and smoking a cigarette. She was still wearing the red boots, and some kind of short black dress with a thick belt cinched around her waist. In the kitchen light she looked less like a skeleton and more like a tired model with delicate narrow wrists and puffy eyes and bright red lips. Her nails were painted dark purple—like perfect moons. I thought her nail polish would be chipped. It wasn't. It was flawless.

Hi, I said.

She looked up at me. She looked down at her glass.

Do you want some whiskey?
Okay.

She turned around and pulled another glass down from the cabinet. She poured whiskey into both glasses and handed me one. The glass had a film of dust around it. I took a sip and my throat stung. I took another sip.

Do you live here? I asked the girl.
Sometimes.
I'm Noelle. I held out my hand. She held it limply.
Dana.

We stood there for a while. She smoked. I looked at my glass.

You're with Parker? she finally said.

I didn't know what to say. It occurred to me that he might not say yes if someone asked him if he were with me. In fact, he probably wouldn't say anything.

Sort of.

Dana looked down at her glass. She smiled. I was kind of surprised to see her smile. It made her seem more something. More human.

One can only ever sort of be with Parker.

I remembered her staring at me the first night. Suddenly my skin felt cold.

What do you mean?

She looked up. Her face had softened suddenly. I wanted her to tell me things. I wanted to tell her things. I felt, right then, like Dana was going to tell me something very true and important and maybe even become my friend.

Oh, don't worry. I don't mean I'm sleeping with him or anything. Not anymore, she said.

My throat closed.

Parker has been my friend for a long time. I love Parker. But I'm not his girlfriend.

Oh.

Parker's just complicated. You're never going to get a whole lot of him.

I took another sip of my whiskey. My hand was shaking.

I mean, physically he'll act like he wants to give you anything you want, but emotionally he won't give you an inch. You know?

Dana laughed. It occurred to me that I should feel threatened by her, but I felt thankful.

Yeah, I know, I said. I thought it was me.

Dana held out her pack of cigarettes. I took one.

It's not you. It seems like he likes you.
How can you tell?

She lit my cigarette.

The way he looks at you.
Yeah?
Here's the thing about Parker, Dana said. He'll make you feel really beautiful one second…

And like you're not even there the next?

She smiled again.

Yeah. But listen, Noelle, I'm just telling you the truth. He's my friend. There's something about him. It's like, he just has this something about him.

I know, I said. I held out my glass. Can I have some more whiskey?

Dana emptied the bottle into both of our glasses. Then she held hers up.

To Parker, she said.
Cheers.

Nadio

Come with me to the soup kitchen, I said at breakfast.

Noelle looked up from her coffee mug. She pushed her hair back and stared at me.

Keeley, who'd just come in the side door, turned from the tea kettle she was watching on the stove.

Okay, they both said at the same time.

I don't know why I was surprised. I was the one who asked. But I wasn't sure where it had come from. I hadn't been there since Molly left, since before the summer. I'd definitely never brought anyone with me. But that

Saturday morning it felt like what I wanted to do. I wanted to remember all of the things I'd spent my time on before.

Cool, I said. We leave in twenty minutes.

In less than an hour we were climbing the stairs at the St. Francis Community Center. It was still early and folding tables lined the back wall. A few volunteers were placing chairs at round tables around the room and Ben, who was the pastor who ran the soup kitchen, was lifting a steaming dish onto the back table. His gray beard swam behind the steam coming up from the dish. Keeley and Noelle stood next to me, hands pulled up inside their sleeves. I'd never noticed they both stood that way, kneading their fingers into the ends of their sleeves.

Hey, I said. Carol.

Carol looked up from the back of the room. Her glasses slid low on her nose. Carol was in her sixties and she and Ben had helped start the soup kitchen after the Vietnam war about a hundred years ago when, she'd told me once, there seemed to be a flood of men who couldn't keep a home and needed a hot meal. She waved to me and walked slowly over.

We've missed you, young man, she said.

I'm sorry. This year has been...

But we're glad you're here now.

Carol was never one for excuses. She wanted volunteers however she could get them.

You must be the twin sister. She held her hand out and Noelle took it.

And the best friend, Carol said, each of her hands holding one of theirs. Come this way and we'll get you two started on the biggest vat of fruit salad you've ever seen.

As the three of them walked away I could see them laughing. I hadn't seen that in such a long time—Noelle laughing and Keeley laughing and all of us in one place doing something that felt like normal and wasn't about all of these things we were trying to keep from each other.

Well, he's back. Ben handed me an oversized dish of lettuce and pale tomatoes and pointed to the end of the table.

I'm sorry I haven't been around this year, I said. I hadn't anticipated all the guilt I was suddenly feeling. We had never attended church once in our lives and Lace had raised us without a suggestion of religious faith, but two years ago I'd answered a call for volunteers on a sign posted outside the church and Ben had become my unofficial mentor, teacher, maybe even father figure (I'm sure he knew about Molly). But that last part I might be imagining.

Just glad to see you now, he said.

Your sister? He nodded his head toward Carol, handing me a paper bag of bread.

Yeah, I said. And her—my—

Ben raised his eyebrow.

My girlfriend. Keeley.

Ben nodded.

Let's get this sliced, he said. He handed me a serrated knife and we stood side by side, hacking at the mostly stale loaves.

Actually, I said, she's my sister's best friend too.

Ben sliced.

But my sister doesn't really know about us—it's like, it happened sort of unexpectedly, me and Keeley. I guess when you know someone for a long time, it's kind of shocking when you start to see her in a totally different light. You know?

Ben smiled.

> This is an important time in your life, he said.
> You mean—?
> I simply mean it's an important time.
> Yeah, I said. I hoped he wasn't talking about sex. I had the feeling he wasn't but I couldn't be sure.
> Anyway. My sister doesn't know.
> I imagine that feels very difficult for both of you.
> Well, yeah. We're—I think we're figuring out how to tell her.

Even though Ben didn't say anything, even though he just nodded and raised one eyebrow at a time, I felt somehow better.

Carol lined me and Noelle and Keeley up behind the service table. Lasagna, salad, bread. Noelle, Keeley, me. We didn't say much, but Noelle and Keeley giggled into each others shoulders as the old men flirted with them and it was kind of nice to watch.

Noelle

Hey, how about I cook for you? he asked.

We were tangled together on the couch, his face against my neck. I was as usual struggling to decide how far I could let this go. Wanted to let this go.

Really? All the muscles in my stomach, chest, arms, every muscle seemed to flood slowly out into the couch. Relaxed.

Yeah, he said. He sat up.

Yeah, I snagged some stuff from the restaurant. I wanna try something.

Okay, I said. I'd love that.

He stood up, pressing down on my leg as he did. Then he stopped, looking down at me.

One catch, he said.

What?

You gotta stay like that. No putting your shirt back on.

I looked down. My stretched-out black bra, dotted with tiny gray lint pills. My skin was white-blue already against the cool air of the room.

It's cold, I said. Not to mention I felt ridiculous. Which I didn't say out loud.

Too bad, he grinned, walking away. You look hot, he said and walked into the kitchen.

I sat up. The white skin of my stomach rolled just slightly over the waist of my jeans. I knew I wasn't fat, but the waist of my jeans cut just exactly wrong into the skin of my stomach. I decided I wouldn't sit down. In my socks and jeans and old bra, I padded into the kitchen.

Parker had his head inside the fridge. He pulled out a few plastic bags filled with leaves and turned around.

Okay, he said. He was smiling. I couldn't remember

ever seeing him smile that way. He opened the cabinet and pulled a giant book down.

What are all of these plants? I asked, pointing at the tiny pile of plastic bags as he flipped through the pages.

Herbs, he said, not looking up.

And that? I touched the top of the book.

My bible, he said. Suddenly he snapped the book shut, tucked it back in the cabinet and turned to fill a pot with water.

You don't need the recipe?

Nah, I never use recipes. I was just checking something.

I opened the cabinet door and looked at the spine of the book. *Larousse Gastronomique* was etched into the spine.

I watched Parker pouring from a bag into the pot of water.

What does that mean? I pointed at the spine of the book. I felt like a four-year-old.

He looked up, like he was surprised someone else was in the room with him.

Oh, it's like a dictionary for cooks. It's like—you can

look up ingredients and stuff. It's like this old French thing.

As he reached for a knife, the inked band around his arm waved slightly, the serpent danced against his skin. I thought right then that I might be in love with him. I had no idea what that felt like. But right then I decided I could move into this gasoline apartment and do my homework while he read French cookbooks and I wouldn't be missing anything in my life. At all.

Hey, he said. Come stir this for me.

We were mostly quiet while Parker cooked. There was the jump of his knife against the cutting board and the hiss of boiling water and the snap of the containers he opened. I started to forget that I wasn't wearing a shirt. I was stirring risotto, which is little oval-shaped Italian rice that takes forever to cook and needs to be carefully stirred, constantly. The steam from the pot warmed my chest and I didn't care when my arm started to ache. Every once in a while Parker would reach over me to drop a handful of herbs or powder into the pot and each time he did, I felt my skin stand up. It was like he just, instinctually, knew things—the perfect pinch of ingredients or turn of the flame. Watching him cook I could feel he just knew.

On the burner next to me, he poured cream into a pot, a pat of butter, red flakes of something, onions, and handfuls of soft, white meat tinged in red.

What is it? I asked.
Lobster.

People didn't eat lobster on any normal day. This I knew. It was the most expensive thing on a menu. It was special-occasion food.

When Parker proclaimed the risotto done, it was almost too tired to stir, white and gloppy and flecked with dark green and pepper. He heated butter in a pan and formed the risotto into full-moon patties and cooked them until they were gold on each side.

He smiled while he stirred and flipped and sliced and his eyes, all at once, seemed to be watching every pot and dish he had with this quiet, still intensity.

He pulled out two chipped china plates. I thought it was funny, just then. Parker had dishes. Where did he get them? I watched his hands move quickly—stirring, flipping. He put two of the gold-brown risotto patties on each plate, carefully side by side and then, slowly and gently, poured the red cream over the top, so gently that tiny heaps of lobster meat formed a near-perfect pyramid between the two cakes.

He put the plates on the table and stared at them.

Oh, he said. He reached into a drawer and pulled out two forks. Handing one to me, he sat down.

Okay, he said.

I sat down across from him. This is what we would do if we lived together. We would eat dinner like this.

Except I'd probably be fully dressed.
Or maybe not.
I took a bite. Parker watched me.

Wow, I said. I had no idea what to say. It tasted amazing. It tasted warm and creamy and rich and peppered and just a little bit crispy all at once.

It's so good, I said. It's really rich.

Parker stared at me.

Huh, he said.

He took a bite.

Yeah, it's pretty good, he said. I overdid it on the heavy cream.

No, no you didn't.

I had no idea what it would taste like if he underdid it on the heavy cream, but I had the distinct impression I couldn't say anything right. I liked food. But I didn't know food. I wanted to know everything. I wanted to stun him by tasting exactly the spices and the measurement of heavy cream.

I wanted to know what *gastronomique* meant.

Nadio

There was this scholarship. It was for a summer-long Model U.N. program in New Haven, Connecticut. You had to submit your best resolution, and then a committee reviewed millions of them and chose a couple of students to send to New Haven and paid for everything and gave you money for college. It was the kind of thing I should want to do. It was the kind of thing I would have been all over last year. Mr. Taylor, my guidance counselor, pulled me aside right around Thanksgiving and told me I had to get it done.

Just do it, Nadio, he said. It's a waste not to do it. Just get it done.

He was right. It was a Friday, but after school I went straight to the library. I sat down at a computer near the back windows and I just went to it. I knew I was supposed to write about the development of programs to recognize kids orphaned by AIDS. I surfed around and did a little bit of research. It was pretty easy once I got started. I had the format down. It was all about phrasing.

Noting: that children on the continent of Africa have been ravaged by the plague of AIDS, left homeless and orphaned and have resorted to crime and addiction.

Deeply concerned: that the international community has done little to remedy this plight.

Taking into account: that children and countries will be best served by programs that can allow these orphans to grow up with safe, healthy environments on their home soil.

Requests: that delegates develop U.N.-sponsored homes and programs for said orphans.

I stopped. Deeply concerned. Taking into account. It was everything we were thinking about my sister. It was all of my energy and all of my distraction.

Noting: that Noelle is in a weird place. She seems angry and messed up and is keeping her distance from her brother and her best friend.

Deeply concerned: that Noelle could be really hurt if she finds out her brother and her best friend are dating. Kind of dating.

Taking into account: that her brother and best friend really like spending time together and are tired of keeping secrets.

Requests: that all three have a conversation so all of this can stop driving everyone slightly crazy.

I dug my cell phone out of my pocket and called Keeley.

> Hello?
> I wanna take you out to dinner, I said.

She was quiet.

> Really?
> Yeah.
> Nadio. That would be—okay. That's awesome.
> If we're gonna go into the city we have to take the
bus. You know Lace hasn't taken me for my road test yet.

She laughed.

I have a license, remember?

This is humiliating, I said. But can you pick me up at the library?

Which part? That you're at the library or that I have to drive you around?

Ha ha, I said.

Keeley and I drove to Mirabel's. It's just a little restaurant in the city that looks kind of fancy from the outside with dark purple tablecloths and wine glasses, but it's not that expensive. I know because once Lace took us there for her birthday.

Anyway, Keeley and I went to Mirabel's and they gave us a table in the back corner which was actually near the fireplace. We both ordered steak and ice water and Keeley made me promise we would split the check. I didn't argue. To be honest, I couldn't argue. I just wanted to be somewhere brand new with her.

She held my hand over the table.

You want to talk about something, don't you? she said.

In fact, I said.

Do you want to break up with me?

No, I said. Even though I think she knew that wasn't what I wanted.

This is weird, I said. I moved my hand so it was over hers.

It's just…okay. First, I think keeping this from Noelle is ridiculous. I mean, she is my sister and she's your best friend and this is just the truth. She needs to know.

What's the truth?

What do you mean?

Well, you said "this" is the truth. What's "this"?

You and me, Keeley. You're my girlfriend. That's the truth.

She smiled, but there was something off about her smile.

I like to hear you say that, she whispered.

What's wrong?

She lowered her eyes. She wriggled her fingers and then laced them through mine.

I'm not sure when I'm gonna be ready to have sex with you.

My stomach jumped. For some reason it felt weird to hear her say this out loud. It's like we weren't supposed to talk about this out loud.

Okay, I said. But—
Why? she asked.

Yes, I wanted to say. Why? Why not? What are we waiting for? What am I supposed to do here? But I didn't say anything.

There's just all this stuff. And Nadio, I just can't tell you about it all yet but I want to. And sometimes it's like I want to so bad. Do it. Tell you. Everything. But then I don't. But then being with you is like the best thing. I just have to ask you to be patient with me. But I understand if you can't.

Of course I can, I said.

Because I could. Even if I didn't always feel like it. I had no idea what she was talking about. And I couldn't tell if it was serious or just a girl thing—just a girl not being ready. Being ready, I know, is just different for a girl. I knew I could wait. At least right now I felt like I could.

Anyway, she said.

Just then the waiter hovered over us. He grinned as we pulled our hands apart. He put the plates down in front of us—two giant brown steaks, piles of mashed potatoes, hills of green spinach.

Keeley picked up her knife and fork.

Anyway, I love you, she said, slicing into her steak. And you don't have to say anything. In fact, don't say anything. Even if you mean it. Say it a different time when it doesn't feel like you're being forced to say it.

And she shoved her fork in her mouth. She smiled and chewed at the same time, looking kind of beautiful and crazy all at once and I thought, even if I couldn't say it, I might mean it.

We never got back to talking about Noelle.

Noelle

After he cooked, Parker seemed distracted. He piled the dishes in the sink and didn't seem to notice when I put my T-shirt back on.

Thanks, he said when I started to do the dishes. Seriously.

He lit a cigarette, offering his pack to me. I shook my head. He sat down and smoked quietly. I washed and piled the dishes and he was quiet. I felt this strange mix of content and anxiety. Like he'd just showed me this deep and true part of him and we were closer. And like I'd reacted all wrong and he didn't want me around.

I finished the dishes. Even though it was Friday, it was

kind of late and I didn't have a cover plan and I had to go home. I got my stuff from the couch. He had his big French cooking bible out and was flipping through it.

I have to go, I said.

Yeah. Parker looked up. He stubbed out his cigarette and stood up. He watched me pull on my shoes and zip my coat. Then he reached his arm out and pulled me to him and tilted my face up and kissed me.

I felt like I could fly.

You're good to cook for, he said.
You're a good cook.

He smiled.

I'll see you, he said.

It was cold outside, the just-before-the-snow kind of cold. The air felt sharp and fresh on my face as I started toward the bus stop. I felt like I'd cracked open and had a brand new skin and something completely new was going to happen in my life. I felt possible.

That's when I saw them.

Just across from the bus stop there's a restaurant that

Lace took us to once for her birthday. An old-fashioned lamp hooks yellow light over the doorway. As I came up the street a couple was standing under the light. They were wrapped around each other, kissing, wound up so it was hard to tell where one body stopped and the other one started. The woman pulled her head back. She was laughing. Her hair fell down her back under a white hat. Her hair was long and caught the light—gold.

Keeley.

As she tipped her head back and the two bodies separated, I saw both of their faces.

Keeley. Nadio. Keeley and my brother.

I think I stopped breathing for just a second. Or maybe I was numb. Or maybe there was not a single thought in my head.

And then all at once I thought I wanted to throw up.

And then my eyes were filled with tears.

And then I raged with anger.

And then I ducked into the closest alley.

I leaned back against the cold wall. I couldn't catch my breath. It was like I'd been running.

What did I just see?

I wiped at my cheeks. The tears felt cold and stung and I was furious at them.

What was happening? I couldn't move. I didn't dare look back into the street.

I dug in my bag for my cell phone.

Hello? Jessica yelled. There was music in the background.

I need you to pick me up downtown, I said.

Noelle?

Yeah. I need you to pick me up downtown. I need to sleep over.

Is everything okay?

Yeah, I said. Please.

There were muffled voices.

Okay, Jessica said. Okay, I'll be there in ten minutes.

I hung up and called Lace. I told her I was spending the weekend at Jessica's.

I leaned back against the wall. I closed my eyes. I tried to slow my breath.

I felt like I'd cracked open all over again and now I was spilling everywhere.

Nadio

Dear Dario,

I was ready to tell my sister that Keeley and I were, whatever we were. I was ready to just tell her and get on with our lives, somehow the way they'd been. But after that dinner, after that moment when Keeley said something to me I never thought about hearing, I didn't want to tell anybody about it. It's hard to explain. All the other stuff just became less important. I just wanted to be with Keeley. I just wanted to figure it out with her. Maybe that's what you felt like. Maybe you felt like this so much, you couldn't think about sharing Lace with anyone. Not even us. I think I got a glimpse of that. It scares the hell out of me.

It's funny. You'd think that if your girlfriend tells you

she has no idea when she'll be ready to have sex with you, it wouldn't really do wonders for your relationship. But somehow, it made everything sort of solid between us. It was like from the moment Keeley cut into her steak at Mirabel's, we became something different. I knew she was beautiful, anyone who walked by her on the street knew that. I knew that sometimes I couldn't stop thinking about her—the way she breathed under my ear before she kissed my neck or pulled my belt loops into her. But then I started to think about her chewing her steak and laughing at the same time and telling me she loved me without letting me say a word. There weren't a lot of girls I knew who would be brave like that and then just let you watch them chew a giant mouthful of food.

Keeley wanted us to just be open about everything. She was waiting for me outside the soup kitchen on Sunday.

Do you want a ride home? she asked.

Do you think we should? I don't want Nole to see us. She hasn't been home all weekend and it might be weird if—

Keeley hadn't been over to our house since the soup kitchen day.

Jesus, Nadio. She was leaning against the side of her car, her arms folded. How long are we going to do this? she asked.

What do you mean?

THIS. Pretend like we're not together. Walk on eggshells around Noelle. Let her be in charge of everyone's lives 'cause we're all scared of her.

I'm not scared of her, Keeley. I just feel like she's going through enough right now.

Enough of what? Enough of being a selfish brat. Enough of skipping school for some boyfriend no one's ever seen? Enough of denying happiness to the people she cares about because she doesn't have any?

Whoa.

Well. Keeley uncrossed her arms and rubbed her hands together. I'm sorry, Nadio, but it's true. I just feel like Noelle is dominating our whole relationship and she's not even in it.

I think there is a lot of other stuff that dominates our relationship too, I said. I couldn't help it.

Keeley's eyes got wide. She took a deep breath.

Okay, she said. That's fair.
I'm just saying—

You're saying it's not all about Noelle.

It's not, I said. She's my twin sister and my instinct is to protect her. But this is weird. For the first time I have an instinct to protect someone else too.

I hope you're talking about me, Keeley said. She smiled.

So how're we gonna do this? I asked.

We have to talk to her, Keeley said.

But when we got home, she was asleep. Lace said she had a fever.

Noelle

I spent the weekend at Jessica's in a state of near-living. That's all I can say. I was walking around but it wasn't like it was my body or even my head. I couldn't believe things. I felt like something had happened that changed the way I saw everything. I couldn't stop thinking, can I really be this alone? I felt like there was nothing but cold air around me. Like if I opened my mouth nothing would come out, nothing anyone could hear. Even though I was at Jessica's, it was like complete solitude. I just lay on her bed and stared at the television. I held my phone in my hand. Call me, call me, I whispered in my head, till it became a rhythm.

Who was I talking to? Parker, my brother, Keeley. I didn't even know.

What did I see? What happened? Were they really a couple? For how long? They were kissing like it was something they did all the time. The way she laughed up at him was a way I'd never seen her. And Nadio. I'd never seen that much affection from him, the way he held on to her. I'd never seen that ever.

I thought, I thought, I thought. I thought Parker was my secret. I thought I would have this secret relationship, I'd get something no one else felt yet, no one else knew, and it would be all mine and I would get to have this other life too. I would get something.

Now I couldn't even call him. I couldn't.

So what? he'd say about my brother and Keeley. All of us are free to decide, he'd say. The two of them together aren't about you. So what?

But it was about me. It was. All I wanted was for him to see that. And fill in that space.

Jessica thought Parker and I had had a fight. She rubbed my back and brought me cups of tea. It's all right, she said. You guys'll work it out. I let her think so. I couldn't explain anything else to her. I felt paralyzed and broken at once. The only way Jessica could explain that was through Parker.

Why don't people ever see the way other kinds of love can wreck you? What about the way being left out of love can wreck you?

Everything always happened for Nadio. For Keeley. Being beautiful, seeing places. Winning awards. It just happened. Now there was no room.

*   *   *

It came to me on Sunday. I told Lace I was sick and faked a fever. I went straight to my room and didn't see my brother. On Monday morning she called me in sick without even an argument. I slept through the morning after she went to work. I took a shower and shaved my legs and tried to find nice underwear but it was all cotton and sort of faded. So I picked a red-pink pair and the lacy tank top and I got dressed and took the bus to his house.

I knew he was working but the door was never locked,

not through Sammy's. The clean dishes I'd piled in the sink were still there. There was an ashtray overflowing on the kitchen table and a T-shirt tossed over the back of a chair, but otherwise Parker's apartment looked like a set—barren and unlived in and waiting.

I could live here. I could live here.

I imagined my sweaters piled on the empty shelf in his closet. I touched the sleeves hanging there. I imagined my textbooks next to his cookbooks on the bookshelf. Lace had been seventeen, a year older than me, and living alone in another country, living and eating and sleeping with the person she loved. I could do it.

I lay down on his bed, on top of the sheet and a tangled blanket and I pulled his T-shirt against my neck. I pulled my knees up to my chest.

I wanted to be just here.

When he woke me up it was dark outside. He was sitting on the couch and put his hand on my arm.

Hey.

I opened my eyes.

What are you doing here?

I wanted to see you, I said, barely awake, groggy enough to admit this out loud.

Okay, he said. His eyes were narrow, puzzled, but soft. It's a school night, he said. And it's late.

I don't care, I said.

I could see behind him. The night was black outside. I reached up and pulled the collar of his jacket down to me. I kissed him. I tried to swallow him. I dug my fingers into the back of his neck. I could feel him pushing back into me, all of him. I moved my hands down under his T-shirt. His skin felt strange and familiar at once. He stretched and bent until all of him was on top of me like a blanket. I knew what his body was going to do. That was suddenly familiar. Everything was reaching and immediate. I moved my hands to his belt, digging into my hip. I fumbled at it. I could feel the wires and muscles in all of his limbs tense and strong at once. My hand stumbled, his belt pressed into my hip. He pushed my hand away and undid his belt in a moment, a second—he pushed my hand back toward the waist of his jeans then as his fingers flipped back to my stomach, my zipper. My skin jumped. His mouth fought against mine. Our jeans peeled down almost at once. The skin of my legs against his skin. His hands kneaded at me. He lifted his head.

You okay?

I nodded. I had nothing left to say out loud.

As I nodded everything happened like a waterfall—fierce, rushing, crashing. Our clothes gone, it was just skin and the strength of his arms and hands against me and the heat from his skin. We ripped and pulled at each other and pushed against each other. He held my head back and kissed my neck and my fingers pushed his back and we breathed. I stopped thinking at all. I stopped everything that wasn't right there.

And it was over.

It didn't hurt especially. It just was.

He fell asleep. It was almost immediate. Stretched out snake-like, still on top of the twisted sheets, his breaths even and deep. He was sleeping. I sat up. I traced my hands along the designs across his back, and down the length of his spine:

what
does not
destroy me
makes me
stronger

I traced my fingers lightly up and down the letters. Wake up, my head whispered. Wake up.

He did finally. I heard his breathing catch as he came out of sleep and twisted to look at me.

What're you doing, he said. There was nothing in the way he said it. It wasn't sharp or angry or tender or sweet. He was only asking.

What's this one? I asked, my finger against the base of his spine.

He looked at me. He blinked.

It's, uh. It's a reminder.

Of?

It was something I needed to remember at the time. You know? That my family bullshit wasn't going to be... it's my journal entry or whatever. It was that time. It's a reminder. He reached out and squeezed my knee.

You okay? I'm beat. I gotta sleep.

As I began to nod, he turned back onto his side. In seconds his breathing was even, in, out, the perfectly unconscious pattern of sleep.

Nadia

Last night Keeley told me the truth about what happened in Oxford. We went up to her house to study for a Chem exam. Sitting on her couch facing each other, our legs stretched out side by side, she told me the truth about this person who makes her throat close and the muscles in her stomach clench and her skin turn cold even when it's me who is touching her.

The part that I never wanted to say out loud is this: when Keeley was telling it, I could feel what he was feeling. Just for one second, I knew what he felt like.

That's the part I can't get rid of.

I have to tell you something, she said.

About Nole?

No. About me.

Okay.

You're not gonna like it.

Somehow, I knew that before she even said any more.

Okay, I said out loud.

His name was J, she said. But that wasn't his real name. His real name was Jameson something something but he always just went by the first letter.

Jameson what? I pushed. I wanted the details that didn't mean anything. I wanted all of the things she didn't know.

She didn't answer me. I wanted to string her story along. I don't think I really wanted to know how it ended.

She didn't even know his last name. She knew he went by J and she said sometimes she thought he was made out of wax. She said his skin and his joints were like rounded, constantly moving waves and almost seemed carved to perfection.

I couldn't believe she told me that.

Why are you telling me this?

I need you to know it all, she said.

Now?

Yes, now. I'm tired of keeping stuff.

I need all these details?

Please, Nadio. Just listen to me.

She said she met him in a place called Georgina's where she used to sit and read. Georgina's is upstairs in the covered market, with heavy tables and weird thin bagels—it's like a secret hideaway and a hip Oxford student place all at once. And Keeley would sit there and read. On purpose, she said, she read things like *US Weekly* and *Angels and Demons*—things her parents would scoff at and no Oxford student would be caught dead carrying.

She said J found her there. He asked if he could sit with her. This was okay because Georgina's is so small that sharing tables is just part of sitting there. But right away he started talking to her. And he didn't say a word about the magazine she was reading. He nodded at her bagel.

Are you American? he asked her.

Yes, she said.

Only you Americans eat those things.

But he didn't say this with any kind of disdain. She said

his accent was slow-moving and sharp all at once—like a carved-out, deep, booming movie accent. And every time he said anything, he said it with this slow smile that wrapped all the way around her and reached deep inside her like there was suddenly no one else at Georgina's. And Keeley wanted to reach across the table and open her mouth against his and—

She stopped there. She said, You know what I mean, Nadio.

I knew what she meant. I started to feel sick.

Keeley and J were basically never apart after that. For exactly three and a half weeks. The end of it all was what she was leading up to, when she started talking in the living room after everything around us was asleep. It was so deep between night and morning I didn't even know what to call it. I put my hand down over her legs, but she pushed me away, she drew her knees to her chest so we weren't touching at all.

Don't, she said. Don't touch me while I'm telling you this.

I can only remember it in her voice. It's like her voice plays in my head when I think about it.

All along I told him I didn't want to have sex with him, because I don't know, I just didn't think I was ready for it, but sometimes, well, it was like my whole body went against everything I was saying. Anyway. We broke up. He said he couldn't wait around for me to make up my mind, to stop being a child. I was devastated. I thought it was the end, that I'd never actually feel anything ever again. I was so lonely and I didn't have anyone to talk to and I missed him like crazy.

Finally I went to his room. He lived in this small round room in a tower, it was this dark tower with a real twisting stone staircase. I went there and when he opened the door he didn't seem right. Nothing seemed right. He said what? Like he was so mad, like he was spitting almost. I didn't have anything to say. I'd gone there to say I was sorry and I wanted to try to work things out but when I saw him, I couldn't say it. It was like he'd turned into someone else completely. He was like all rage. We stood there staring at each other and then he kinda laughed. You want this? he said. And he grabbed my arm and pulled me inside the room. It was like he was possessed. I could still feel the burning on my arm where his fingers dug in but then he just threw me down and he was on top of me.

You know, I can't remember if I made a sound. I remember pushing at him. I remember trying to get him off of me but I don't think I could make a sound. It was like I was fighting him on mute. I swear to god. It was like of all the noise in the room there was no sound. That's what I have now, it's like this soundless memory. And everything he did was like straight from his rage. I couldn't believe it was happening. Like this. It was so fast. My clothes were even all on after it was over. And J. He wouldn't even look at me. He was just lying on his back, staring up at the ceiling. My whole body felt, just like cracked, like stiff, like—somehow, I don't even know, I got up and I straightened everything out on me and walked out and once I hit the street, it's like all the sound came back.

She stopped. She wasn't breathing in or out. She stared at her knees. Then she took a deep shaky breath. She just looked up and into my eyes. She was folded up around herself and her hands were shaking.

Can I come over there now? I said. My chest was going to explode.

She nodded. I moved down the couch and I put my arms around her and she felt still and small and tense, everything about her knotted except her shaking hands. I'd never felt anything like the pounding in my chest and the rushing heat in my throat and my ears. I pulled Keeley onto my lap.

I don't cry about it, she said into my neck, her voice barely audible.

I knew I had to say something. She wanted me to say something.

It's okay, I said.
I haven't even talked about it.
Okay. I held her head under my chin. I knew there must be something beyond the top of her head but I couldn't see.
I can't cry about it. I just, I don't want to think about it anymore.
Okay.

I kept saying okay. But I knew I couldn't stop thinking about it. I thought, this is what people mean when they say "animal instinct" because I knew that rage would be stronger than my mind if anyone tried to hurt her, and nothing in the world could make me let go of her.

Noelle

By the time I got back from Parker's it was after dinner and Lace had realized I wasn't sick, not even close. Only I didn't care. She sat me down at the table and started yelling. It was like she suddenly out of nowhere became some other kind of mother, like the ones on television shows who wore pressed skirts and soft sweaters. Out of nowhere Lace started to talk about rules and the way things would be now.

> One, no more going out, she said.
> Like grounded? I asked.
> Not grounding. Just no going out.
> That doesn't even make sense.

Lace took a deep breath. Her hands were knotted together on the table. She stared at me.

The only thing that doesn't make sense right now is your behavior. I give you all the freedom a kid could ask for, Noelle. And it's not working. Now I'm going to have to make sure I know where you are and what the hell you're doing.

So now you don't trust me? I pushed.

I think you've made that impossible. She stared. And school, she said. You go, that's it.

You think I'm not going to school?

Apparently not. And, Noelle, school is not optional. It's not something you get to decide whether or not you'll do. You go to school.

I stared back. I didn't say a word. She went on. She said we needed to make the time to sit down as a family. I stopped listening.

Okay okay okay, I told her. I didn't know how long she'd been talking.

Okay. I didn't feel like fighting. I was so goddamn tired. I hadn't seen my brother but I knew now I could pretend like he didn't exist.

Was my body supposed to feel different? Was my life supposed to feel different? Wasn't it all supposed to begin from here? Was our relationship supposed to be different? Wasn't everything?

What was definitely different was my brother and Keeley. Or not. What was different was that I knew the truth now. I didn't want to think about how long they'd been making everything a lie. I just wouldn't talk to them. It was that simple. I pretended they weren't even there.

*   *   *

When you're a little kid, you don't second-guess what your future is going to look like. There are no questions. Doubts. Not about any of it. Keeley was never not going to be my best friend. She was never not going to be my future. The day before we started high school, we decided to camp out. Nadio wanted to sleep out with us but we wouldn't let him. We pitched a tent on the rise between both of our houses—you could see the living room lights from each house from the door of our tent. We stocked it with quilts and pillows and chocolate chip cookies and magazines and pens and mini iPod speakers and we lay side by side with our flashlights trained on each other.

Everything happens in high school, Keeley said.

You think?

It has to. It's a whole other world.

Like what?

Like people start to treat us like adults. Like we find out where we fit. Like we get to start dating.

Dating, I said. Who?

You know. The high school is bigger. More people from more towns.

Yeah, I said. It was hard to believe.

We were quiet. We were both afraid of the same thing.

Nole?

Yeah.

The first one to get a boyfriend, we have to tell the other one everything. I mean everything.

We don't have to worry, I said.

Why?

It'll happen at the same time. Everything happens to us at the same time. It's like we're blessed that way.

Nadio

Dear Dario,

I actually didn't think much about my sister never coming home. I wished she didn't spend so much time with Jessica Marino, and I knew there was something about her that made me feel worried, but it wasn't until I heard Lace yelling at her that I realized this was all bigger. Lace doesn't yell. We don't push her. It's just this quiet agreement we've always had.

Would you notice if your daughter was losing it? Would you care if she called Friday night and said she wasn't coming home? I know Lace was worried about her. I know she told her no more late-night change of plans. What would be different if she had a dad? You know, I keep thinking that maybe if I'd had someone to talk to about all of this, then it would have all come out of my head and I'd have had the space to notice my sister. Half of all of this is your fault. It has to be.

The other part of this is Keeley. Because how do I know how to be with her now? How do I know how to take care of her and not be him and let us go forward so she can forget about what he did to her? And what about this part of me who understands how he felt. What about that part? I know that comes from you.

I look at both of them, Keeley and my sister, and I think of the kind of people who can ruin them and it scares me.

I wasn't sure how to be with Keeley when she picked me up for school. I felt like part of me had become another person—filled with all this anger and concern. She leaned over to kiss me when I got in the car. I know I turned stiff. I didn't mean to, but everything about her suddenly felt fragile.

I'm the same person I was yesterday, she said.
I know. But I'm not.
Yeah, but you're the person I feel safe with.

I wanted to ask her what made her kiss me that first night but I didn't. She drove and I watched her.

I don't want you to be weird around me, she said.

Well.

Nadio, I'm not made of glass. I want to get past this.

She pulled into a parking spot and turned off the car.

Have you talked to anyone?

You.

You know what I mean.

Keeley sighed. She reached out and held my hand.

I'm okay, she said. If I feel like I'm not, then I'll talk to someone. It happened. Something bad happened to me. And I wish the first time I had sex was different. But I can't let that be who I am.

You sound pretty certain, I said. I couldn't stop thinking that she was trying to pretend this was smaller than it was. I imagined her nightmares, the ones she wouldn't talk about. Keeley pulled her hand away. It was like she knew what I was thinking.

Look, I said. I'm just saying that you sound like you

have it all figured out. But it's okay to let this mess you up.

She looked back at me.

I know, she whispered. But I really feel okay right now.

I pulled Keeley's head against my chest. I held her and she leaned into my neck. Her hair smelled like a woodstove and raspberry. I could feel her heart beating against my arm. I knew that I couldn't save anybody— that my sister, Keeley, even my mom, only they knew what they needed to be okay, to forget or remember, but right then I felt like I wanted to save Keeley from all of it.

And I felt like I could.

Noelle

The weird thing was, I didn't really want to do it again. I sort of thought having sex once would make me know everything about it. But I was still scared to do it again.

But I wanted him to want to do it again.

With me.

Only he didn't call.

I waited until the weekend and then I called him. He didn't answer. It was two days before he sent me a text that said:

Hey.
Having people over tonight.
Been thinking of you.
Come.

The first two lines made my stomach hurt.

But the second two lines were all I needed.

He knew it was a school night. But I had to go. I had to. At the same time, I sort of felt like I shouldn't go alone. I'd been going to Parker's house for three months. It was mine more than anything else. But tonight I didn't want to go alone. Even though Jessica was working, she said I could stay at her house. I begged and pleaded and faked a Government project that needed work and Lace finally let me go.

So I took the bus. I went alone.

Sammy's was closed. Dim lights dripped out from Parker's second floor apartment. The music was low, bumping. I climbed the metal staircase and let myself in.

A few people were sitting around the kitchen table playing cards. A low ceiling of smoke hung just over their heads. Some of them nodded, mumbled, looked back to their cards and drinks. I crept down the hallway. Parker was in the living room. Jessica's brother was there, two other guys I didn't know. Dana.

Hey, Dana said.
Hi.

Nodding. Mumbling.

Parker stood up. He kissed me quickly. It was one-sixteenth of the kiss I wanted.

I sat down on the floor at his feet. There was nowhere else. He put his hand on the back of my neck. I breathed a sigh of relief. In a second it was gone.

The two guys must have worked with Parker. One of them was leaning in, breathless.

...and she was like, these are NOT sweet potatoes. You dyed these with food coloring. You think I'd be fooled? I'm like, LADY. Nobody in our kitchen is gonna go through the trouble of dying real potatoes. Unbelievable. Meanwhile, the woman sent her steak back THREE times. Lady, you can get beef jerky at the gas station...

It's all about back of the house, I'm telling you, Parker said.

Dana was watching me. When I caught her eye she looked away.

Hey, man, are you thinking about Santo's offer in Boston?

He was looking at Parker. Parker was behind me. I turned around.

Boston?
It's nothing. Parker looked at me. He looked at Dana. He looked at the guy.
Never mind, the guy said.

Silence.

Our chef is moving to this place in Boston. He asked—whatever, it's nothing, Parker said.

I'd turned back around so I was facing the room. His voice sat over my head.

Hey, said Dana, I'm gonna open this bottle of wine. Who wants some?

It was like being at his house for the first time, like I was a stranger.

Like I wasn't supposed to be there.

I felt it in my gut all night. I tried to breathe it away.

I tried not to need him. I tried to talk to all the people I didn't know. I tried to talk to Dana but she kept finding excuses—to answer her phone, go to the bathroom, get another drink. She darted her eyes and stretched strange smiles.

I got too high.

I fell asleep on the couch.

I sat up slowly. Looking around.

The room was filmy and dim. Restaurant guy was asleep on the recliner. Bottles scattered across the floor. Parker was nowhere. I started to feel sick. I put my feet on the floor, leaning forward. The coffee table was littered with ashtrays, empty cigarette packs, DVDs, a pile of change and three white pills.

I don't know what made me grab the white pills. I shoved them in my pocket.

Slowly I tiptoed to Parker's room.

He was there. Asleep in his clothes across the sheets. Alone.

I stared at him. My sadness was desperate.

I lay down. I curled myself against his back.

Parker? I whispered.

Silence.

Parker?

Stillness.

Hey.

He shifted.

Hmm, he said.
I have to go.
Mm-hmm.
Parker? I rubbed my fingers down the back of his neck. I could come with you to Boston.

Silent, still. Then, slowly, he pulled away.

He rolled over and looked at me, his eyes wet with sleep.

Huh?

I mean it. I put my hand on his stomach. I have winter break coming up and then I could—I could go to school there. We could get an apartment...

Parker blinked. He rubbed his eyes. He pulled away from my hand and sat up slowly and looked down at me.

Hey, he said.

My heart raced. I felt the heat filling my head. I sat up, stumbling off the bed.

Noelle, come on. I mean—
No, I said. No, I get it.

I was walking carefully, then suddenly I was half running down the hall. My bag was on the counter. I picked it up. I shoved my feet inside my shoes.

I knew I was going to be sick.

Parker came into the kitchen. He was barefoot. He rubbed his eyes.

I gotta go, I said. The bus just started running. I

can get to Jessica's before her parents wake up and it'll look like I slept over—just forget whatever I said, okay?

Noelle. Parker rubbed his hand across his stomach. The toe of the black cat inked above his hip bone peaked above his jeans.

Listen. He took a step forward. The table was between us. I think you're really great, I do—

The room tilted and slid.

I just don't think this is what you want it to be—

I gripped the edge of the counter.

I totally want us to be friends. I just don't think this is working like this—

I took the deepest breath I could.

I just don't want you to—

There was no air in the room. He started to move around the table.

I have to go. I backed up. My arm knocked a bottle. It rolled to the floor. Echoed.

Noelle—

It's okay. It's fine. I have to go—I grabbed at the door. It was locked. I turned, clicked, grabbed. It opened. Parker moved closer to the door.

Hey, he said.

No, it's okay. I gotta go.

I floated. I fell. I ran. I stumbled down the stairs.

This was it. That was it.

Here's what I know.

I threw up right outside his door. Then I felt lighter and almost okay. I caught the bus. I went straight to school and got a piece of gum from someone in the first floor bathroom. I washed my face and swallowed the three pills I'd taken from Parker's coffee table and I pulled my hair back and I went to first period.

Nadio

I felt distracted through double-period Chem. I could barely focus. I couldn't stop feeling Keeley's head against my neck. But it wasn't just that. It was like I knew something was wrong. When Mr. Taylor came to the door of the classroom, I knew he was there for me. Only I thought it was about the half-assed job I'd done on my M.U.N. application. I was halfway out the door before he even finished talking to Mr. Donohoe.

Listen, I know it wasn't my best work, I said.

Mr. Taylor looked at me funny.

Nadio, I'm here about your sister.

She's not applying, I said. I had no idea what he was talking about.

Noelle is in my office. Ms. Hayes called me and asked me to remove her from Government class.

What? I was starting to realize this had nothing to do with M.U.N.

She was hysterical. Apparently she disrespected Ms. Hayes and this escalated. Your sister does not seem like herself.

I don't know what you're talking about, I said. He couldn't be talking about my sister.

I've called your mother at work but we're having trouble reaching her. I was hoping you could just sit with your sister and calm her down. I'll give you two my office.

As we went into the guidance offices, Keeley was coming out. She looked at us, her eyes wide.

Hi, I said.
Hi. Wha—
What are you doing here? I asked.
I was meeting with my college counselor, she said, looking at Mr. Taylor.

Mr. Taylor, I said. Let me bring Keeley with me. She's Noelle's best friend. We can help.

Mr. Taylor's eyes darted between us.

Okay, he said. He waved toward his door. She's in there. I'll give you all some space.

Mr. Taylor walked into the college counselor's office. I turned to Keeley.

Apparently she freaked in Government, I said. Hayes kicked her out.

That's not like her, Keeley said. Something's up.

I don't know why I felt so nervous as we pushed into Mr. Taylor's office.

Noelle was slumped down in a chair, her legs splayed out, loose and exhausted looking. She had a hood pulled low over her head, which was resting in her hands. She looked up when she heard the door. Her face was wrecked. There is no other way to say it. I'd never seen her like that. It was red and swollen and tear-streaked and her eyes were framed in heavy shadows. Her hair hung tangled out of the sides of the hood.

Nole … I said. I didn't know what to say next. I was scared of my sister. I didn't recognize anything in her face. I couldn't read a thing. I couldn't feel a thing coming from her.

She stared at us.

Perfect, she said.

Suddenly her eyes seemed to be flaming.

Sweetie, what happened? Keeley said, moving toward her. Noelle held her hand out.

Don't come near me, she said.

Keeley stopped.

And don't call me sweetie. You fucking liar.

She pushed her hood back and sat up straight.

Both of you fucking liars. What did you think? Oh, we'll just have our perfect little honor roll beautiful people pseudo-relationship and dumb Noelle will never know the difference. We'll just grow up into this perfect newspaper reading student government couple and forget about everyone else. We'll just pretend we don't have sisters or best friends or anything else. We'll just have our perfect Oxford trips and scholarships and giggling pathetic romantic dinners and oh, WHO THE FUCK IS NOELLE? Honey, didn't we used to know someone named Noelle? I don't know honey it sounds kind of familiar but everything before Harvard is just a BLUR...

By the end she was yelling, almost spitting her words. Keeley looked like Noelle had slapped her. She was frozen in place.

I felt numb. I felt like a crazy person was standing in my sister's sweatshirt. A true maniac.

Noelle stood up slowly. She walked past Keeley as if she weren't even there. It was like she'd stopped seeing her. She stopped right in front of me. Her face inches from mine.

You are both so fucking selfish, she whispered. I bet you're just like him.

She walked out of the room so soundlessly it was like she simply stopped being there. The air was cold. The only sound was Keeley's quiet crying.

Noelle

You looked wrecked, Jessica said when I walked into Government first period. She offered me eye drops but I waved them away. I dug my sunglasses out of my bag and slipped them on. My eyes were filling and spilling over before I noticed, all the time, before my head could catch up. Eye drops wouldn't help me. Being back in school made everything rush in. Everything I was feeling changed to anger. I was stiff with being mad. By the time Ms. Hayes started lecturing I knew I wasn't going to make it. I knew.

Noelle, sunglasses, Ms. Hayes said, as if she'd just noticed I was there.

Yes, I said. They are.

Off, she said.

I stared at her. I knew she couldn't see my eyes and I narrowed them to glare.

Now, she said. The rest of the class was silent, watching me.

What do you care? I can listen just as well with them on as with them off. I didn't know where this was coming from, who I was, talking to her.

Noelle. We don't wear sunglasses in the classroom. Take them off or it's the principal's office. It's that simple.

I'm not leaving, I said. You're telling me you're going to deny me a history lesson because of sunglasses.

Ms. Hayes took a deep breath. She stared at me.

You're wasting everyone's time, she said. Sunglasses or door, Noelle.

Jessica leaned in to me. Just take them off, she whispered.

But I felt empowered suddenly. For the first time in three days I felt something. I wasn't invisible. Everyone was looking at me.

This is bullshit, I said.

Ms. Hayes already had the classroom phone against her ear. I need Mr. Taylor in Room 209 now, she was saying.

I'm just sitting here listening and you're harassing me because of some bullshit rule. This is great.

Ms. Hayes shook her head. Nobody was moving. Mr. Taylor came in the door and looked at me. Ms. Hayes whispered something to him.

Noelle, he said. I think you need to come with me.

My face was hot. I didn't know where the sound of my voice was coming from. I could see Ms. Hayes' disappointment, embarrassment, all of it. I could see Keeley and my brother...

Forget it, I said. Just forget all of it.

The chair crashed to the floor behind me as I stood up. I didn't mean to knock the chair over. But it crashed and echoed and I felt relieved.

Nadio

When Noelle and I were kids, she was in charge. There was something about her that commanded a room, that made you listen, that drew you in. As we got older, all of this command got quieter and quieter until it slipped away. The only time she was really in charge now was when she was angry. There was something about it—quiet and fierce—that was almost scary. Even to Lace. To me. All of us. It was like the only time she felt confident enough to command was when she was too mad to care.

It was like that in Mr. Taylor's office. She had us frozen.

Keeley and I got Mr. Taylor to let us go look for Noelle.

In the hallway everyone was talking about Noelle in Ms. Hayes' class. It was like they'd never seen her before. They were talking about her like someone else altogether had been kicked out of class.

Whoa, did you hear about Noelle?

Who?

That girl. She never talks. The twin.

The one who hangs out with Jessica Marino?

Yeah. Her. She freaked in Government.

That girl?

Yeah. She told Ms. Hayes off.

No way.

Totally. She was tough. And she looked wrecked.

No, I've seen her. Always with the hood and like she's been out all night.

Did she go here last year?

She was totally different. You just never noticed her.

I heard it all in the hallways. The whispers even lower when I walked by, but I heard it.

Don't listen. Keeley held my arm.

She drove back to my house. We didn't talk.

When I moved toward my front door my stomach started to feel like it had in Chem class. Keeley was behind me, but then she was running up the stairs while I was frozen.

The kitchen table still had this morning's breakfast dishes on it—and in between two coffee cups and a crusty bowl rolled three or four canisters. Prescriptions. Medicine. Empty. Empty pill bottles rolling around on the table.

Nadio. Keeley's voice was quiet and booming and desperate all at once. I took the stairs two at a time. She was kneeling with my sister's head in her lap. Noelle's head was heavy. She was mumbling.

Nadio, call 9-1-1 right now, Keeley said. Quiet. Even.

I dug my phone out of my pocket. I dialed.

My sister, I said. She took pills—

Keeley had to repeat my address to me twice. My hand shook. I hung up.

They're coming.

I stared at my sister lying on the floor. I stared at Keeley holding her head.

Call your mother, Keeley said. Nadio, call your mother and tell her to meet us at the hospital.

The phone weighed fifty pounds. I dialed like I was underwater. I watched.

My sister had stopped mumbling.

She was still.

Noelle

I didn't want to die but everything was over.

It was just over.

That's all I can tell you.

It was easy to find the pills. Lace had a million different prescriptions—to help her sleep, relax, ease her headaches...There was a ceramic bowl that had been filled with grapes. It was on the counter below the phone. I rinsed it out and I poured a glass of water. I don't know what I took from Parker's house, but everything floated in my hands and underneath my skin. I brought Lace's pills from her bathroom. I filled the bowl with the pills. Then I went back to my room. Lace had left a basket of clean laundry on my bed and when I sat down it tipped over. It was warm and soft. I curled up in the cloud of laundry and swallowed the pills in handfuls and sips.

When Keeley and Nadio came home I felt like a balloon was sucking at my head in slow motion. Then nothing. Then there they were again.

Then it's a flash of images in my head, one on top of the other, bright flashes of light, BAM-BAM-BAM. Nadio's big black eyes staring into mine, his hands gripping my shoulders, BAM Keeley yelling, Nadio holding the phone BAM red lights spilling over the wall of my room BAM the black rubber boots and thick veined hands of the ambulance drivers BAM the sound of sirens, a hallway spilling yellow light BAM a man's voice with no body *What did you take, Noelle?* urgent BAM stinging burning down my throat BAM retching black charcoal, strange hands holding at my arms and hair BAM ... and then everything was dark and slow.

When I woke up in the hospital, Lace was asleep. She was sitting in a chair made of shiny green plastic—it looked like a school-bus seat—and her head was leaned forward on the bed, resting against my thigh. She was wrapped in a white blanket, her head turned toward me.

Lace opened her eyes. She stared at me. The silence in the room was heavy. She sat up and the blanket fell off her shoulders. She scooted her chair back and climbed into the bed beside me, wrapping her arms around my neck, lying down next to me.

I'm sorry, she whispered. Sweetie, I'm so sorry.

I felt like I could break into a million pieces. I hugged her back.

I didn't want to die, I whispered.

She pulled my head against her shoulder.

I know, she said.

I was crying. The sobs caught deep in my throat, Lace's shoulder was wet. It had been so long since I felt anything. Now I felt it all at once.

I didn't know what else to do, I said.

Lace was quiet, her hand rubbing my back. I wanted her, I needed her to understand.

Mommy? The word caught in my throat. It didn't

feel right. It was the only thing that felt right. Mom. I didn't know what else to do.

I know, she said.

I felt her shiver. She pulled me against her.

Noelle, when your dad left me my world was broken. I didn't have any parents. I didn't have any family. I just had him. And then he was gone. And I knew I had you two to live for. I never wanted to die. But for a long time I didn't know how I was going to live.

I know, I said. I did. That was it. I didn't know how I was going to live.

The sheets underneath me were scratchy and dry and Lace's skin over her collarbone felt soft and cool. I closed my eyes. I pretended we were at home. I counted the seconds of my breath in and out. I could breathe in this second. I just wanted to get through this second and then the next one. It was okay with my mom. That was enough for now. My body felt heavy and tired. My eyelids felt thick. My throat burned.

Mommy? I said. Saying Lace felt so far away. It felt like what someone else called her.

Mm hmm.

Will you stay here?

Sweetie, I'm not going anywhere.

Nadio

My mom and my sister were asleep on the starched white twin bed when I walked in, Noelle covered in the sheet and Lace next to her, dark colors, their hair twisting together over the pillow. They looked so similar; I don't think I'd noticed it before. Lace could be our age. I sat down in the chair. I didn't know what to do. I'd just walked Keeley to her car, picked up muffins. It was three in the morning and I'd wandered through the white-lit, deserted cafeteria, and it was all I could think to pick up—corn muffins in plastic wrap, made months ago and staring out from the counter beside the register. I bought three. Now I held the muffins and I watched my mom and sister sleep.

Dear Dario,

What I want to know is, what the hell am I supposed to do? Did I let my sister down, should I have seen this, should I get out of here?

In Italy things are very traditional, aren't they? As in the man is in charge and the protector of his family. Does that make me the protector of this family? I wonder what you would feel if you could see my mom and my sister, sleeping in this bare room, looking fragile, both of them. What would you be doing? Or would we even be here right now if you were a part of any of this?

I don't like people very much. I just don't. But I can be whatever I am here with my sister and my mom. And Keeley makes me want to figure out more. She makes me laugh and she makes me want something I never thought about wanting. But right now I feel like there is too much of everything. Like I'm supposed to be giving them all something and I don't know what it is.

And I'm the only one awake around here.

Boo? Lace lifted her head. She was whispering.

Yeah. Are you hungry? I said. I held up a corn muffin.

She looked doubtful. She shook her head, easing herself

out of the bed. Noelle stirred and curled into a ball, her eyes still closed.

Lace walked over to me. She took the corn muffin and kissed the top of my head. She stood over me and held my head against her stomach.

Jesus, she said. Nothing prepares you for this.

I didn't say anything.

Are you okay, Boo?
Yeah.
Really okay?
I'm okay, Lace.
We have to work on this.
I know.
We have to take care of each other.
I know.

We stayed like that for a long time. I think we were both watching Noelle sleep.

Will you watch your sister, Boo? I just want to go get some tea.
Yeah. Of course.

I don't know how long I watched her before Noelle opened her eyes.

Hi, she said.
Hey.

She blinked. She pulled the sheet up to her chin.

I'm sorry, she said.
Don't say you're sorry.
But I am.
I know you are. I pulled the chair over to her bed. I reached up and held her hand over the sheet. I know you're sorry. And I am too.
You're in love with Keeley?

She said it evenly, softly, without accusation or anger. She was asking.

I think I am.

She looked down at my hand, her hand.

It makes sense, she said. I mean, it really makes perfect sense.

She looked up again. Her face was struggling to smile, tears coming out of her eyes.

I think I'm just afraid, she said.

She looked, suddenly, like she'd looked every year of our life. Like she was three and six and eight and eleven and scared somewhere and looking up at me, wordlessly begging me to help her across the river or bear the first day of school. She'd stopped asking for these things with her eyes a long time ago, but there it was again.

I'm just scared of being left.
Okay.

Noelle

My brother said something I think is true. I wasn't scared of being left by him, I was scared of being left behind. Of Keeley living a life I couldn't see. Of not getting to do the things other people got to do. Of not getting a chance.

I don't know. I don't know if that was true. But when he told me Ben wanted him to go to Virginia and help some church family whose house had burnt down, I didn't feel like I was being left behind. When he told me he wanted to go, that he felt like he could help there, like he thought it was important, but he didn't want to desert me, I really and truly wanted him to go.

I just feel like I need to do something, I don't know, physical, he said. Where I can see the help I'm giving.

I got it.

When he told me he thought it would be good for me to spend some time with Keeley, then I wasn't so sure. But I knew he needed to do this. I wanted him to go help somebody else. I wanted him to step outside of helping me.

And I was so tired. I was so tired. I couldn't tell him any more.

I hadn't seen Keeley. I'd been home from the hospital for a few days and I was on medical leave from school. I had all of these assignments and Lace stayed around and watched me eat and read and stare at the TV.

I'm not leaving you, he said. I just need—
I know, I told him. You need to step back. I know.

As scared as I was of everything, I never felt like my brother was bailing on me. I just didn't. He felt like everything was pushing in around him and he needed to step out of all of our space. It was hard, I knew, to be the only man in all of this. I think he felt some responsibility to be a caretaker or a protector—our protector—ancient as it may sound, I think that is what he felt he needed to be. But he didn't know how.

It's fine, I told him.

I really meant it. And I begged Lace to go back to work. I wanted all of them to just give me the space. The emptiness of the house. All of it.

*   *   *

The first day I was home alone I felt like I'd just been introduced to myself, like everything was brand new. I didn't want to live the life I'd been living before but I couldn't get rid of it. It was hard to keep my eyes open. It was hard to get my body to move. I lay on the couch and thought about my clothes. I wanted to wear different things. I didn't want any more worn thin T-shirts. I didn't want to look in the mirror and see my hair stringy and tangled. I didn't want—

I didn't want to think about him, but there he was, pushing on all the edges of every memory.

Keeley came over early in the afternoon. She knocked on the back door and I heard her push it open.

Nole?

But before I could say anything she was standing in the doorway. She looked at me lying on the couch.

Hey.
Hi, she said. She smiled. You look—
It's okay, I said. I look like shit. I know. I can't remember my last shower.
Okay. Can I sit? She wrinkled her nose, smiling. But I'm not gonna sit too close to you.
Sit, I said.

She sat down. Then she stood up. Wait—she said. She opened the shopping bag she was carrying and pulled out two Styrofoam containers.

Grilled cheese and French fries. From the Coyote. Are you hungry?

She held out the container. Suddenly, for the first time in days, I was hungry.

I sat up. It was quiet while we ate our grilled cheese.

Did you skip out on school? I said.

Yeah.

She crossed her legs under her, eating a French fry one tiny bite at a time. We were quiet.

Oh hey, she said. I brought you something. She reached into her bag beside her; digging between notebooks, she pulled out a thick piece of cardstock and extended it out to me. I just wanted, she said, I just—you know, some good memories.

I stared. I could feel my eyes filling and the heat in my cheeks. For the first time in days I felt something. I ran my hand over the smooth photographs, the thick, raised, painted border. I wiped my eyes and I looked up.

Thank you, I said. It's beautiful.

We looked at each other, resting in between smile and discomfort, in between silence and telling. I didn't know what I was ready for, but I was glad she was there.

What do you wanna do? Keeley asked.

In spite of everything, or because of everything, it felt so good to have her sitting there. It felt like a relief.

I wanna clean out my closet, I said.

Let's do it. Keeley's eyes widened. She grinned and jumped up, scooping up both of our empty containers.

But first, you have to take a shower.

Okay. I stood up. I felt shaky. My T-shirt smelled.

Come on. Keeley was two steps ahead of me up the stairs. She went into my room and came out with gray sweatpants and a pink T-shirt I hadn't seen in years.

She pulled a clean towel down from the hall closet.

Go on, she said. I'll find some boxes.

As she headed back down the stairs I fingered the pink T-shirt. I couldn't remember the person who ever wore it. But I kind of couldn't wait to be clean and put it on.

When I came out of the shower, Keeley was in my room, surrounded by empty boxes and a pile of plastic bags.

What's this? I asked her. I scooped my wet hair off my neck, tying it into a bun. My skin felt clean and cold.

Don't you wanna get rid of stuff?

Yeah, I said, suddenly exhausted. I sat down on the bed. All of it.

Keeley moved around the boxes. She sat down on the floor in front of me, crossing her legs.

Let's get rid of it, then, she said.

A drop of water was sliding down my spine, a cool slow-motion crawl.

I don't know when it started, I said. I really don't. All of a sudden you were, like, whipping past me. We'd been on the same road, the same pace, then suddenly you got beautiful. You were going to other countries. I don't know, K... you had like everything and I had nothing. You didn't even want to go to England and I wanted to go anywhere.

It wasn't so great, she whispered. But she didn't sound mad. She was watching me.

I know I haven't been fair, but I felt so left out. Even before I knew about you and Nadio, I think I knew. I just felt like suddenly you had everything. Everyone looked at you when you walked down the hall, and—

Noelle, that's not fair. That's just the way you saw it. And I saw you sneaking around stoned with Jessica Marino not even missing me and I felt totally replaced.

You didn't even need me—

I did. All I did was talk to Nadio about you. And I

was so confused about what was happening with him. I just wanted my best friend—

But you guys didn't even tell me, I said. Our voices were low and pulling. We were desperate, maybe not mad, but desperate.

You weren't even here. And I knew you had something going on with this guy. Nole, I don't even know who he is—you never told me about him.

I tried.

Silence. I stared at the seam of my pants. I reached behind me, rubbing at the water on my neck.

We're gonna change, Keeley said. We're gonna get older and stuff is gonna happen to us—she paused. Something happened to me this summer, she said. And it was like everything I knew was suddenly wrong. Everything safe was suddenly scary. I still don't know—I still feel like I don't know who I am sometimes. But then you remind me. Your brother reminds me. Everything is gonna change but we always have each other. The history of each other. That's who we are.

I slid down off the bed. I sat down next to Keeley and put my arms around her. She leaned her head on my shoulder.

You know, it's funny, I whispered. Parker doesn't know anything about me—he doesn't know you or Nadio or the history of anything.

I could feel Keeley nodding against my shoulder.

But I still—it's like one look from him and I feel like I'm floating.

Yeah, Keeley said.

And then the next second I'm destroyed.

I know.

God, I wish I didn't think about him all the time, K.

It won't always be like that, she said. In a little while you'll only think about him part of the time.

And then a little while after that I won't think about him at all?

Keeley sat up. She squeezed my hand. She wiped away the tears I hadn't even noticed sliding down my cheeks and she smiled.

No, she said. You'll always think about him a little bit.

Nadio

I needed to make a difference in a concrete way. I needed to change something with my hands. I needed to do something for somebody else that I could see. I needed to feel like I could help somebody.

I don't think I ever told Ben any of this directly. But he asked me to drive down to Virginia with him and help repair a house for a family he knew—a house that had been damaged by a fire. Tangible. I had to go. Lace called Mr. Taylor and told him I was invited on this project for church and I could get community service hours for it. Taylor excused me from school—it was just two days. I was getting a lot of breaks at school these days. And he knew I had a 4.0, even now.

I had spent so much time worrying that my sister would feel abandoned that I hadn't stopped to think about Keeley. The night before I was leaving, she called me.

Will you come meet me outside?

Now? I looked out the kitchen window from where I was holding my phone. I could see the lights from her living room cutting holes in the dark slope of hill between us.

Yeah, she said. Please.

Lace and my sister were watching TV, lying with their legs crossing on the couch. I stood in the doorway, zipping my coat.

I'll be right back, I said.

Lace nodded, her eyes on the TV. Noelle looked at me. She nodded. She almost smiled.

Okay, she said. But for a second I thought she said, it's okay.

I turned and my eye caught on something lying on the table by the door. I picked it up. A piece of cardstock, Keeley's hand.

There it was. The photograph of us, in the way I always remembered: a darkened entryway in the Shipleys' living room, the white border of the doorway framing Keeley and my sister—my sister in an orange dress and Keeley in a green dress, laughing and reaching out to each other. Me in the background, the same color as the carpet, watching them. Next to it, a picture I only just then remembered: Noelle, Keeley, me, close to the camera. They were laughing but their eyes were red, I looked serious; a piece of Keeley's hair blew across Noelle's forehead, we were all looking up to where Keeley's arm was outstretched, holding the camera above us. It was the day she left for Oxford. In light green and dark green paints, Keeley had drawn a border of tangled vines linking the pictures together, and at the bottom of the page, in small square print, she wrote: *And here we are.*

I looked back into the living room. Noelle was turned to the TV. I ran my hand along the slick photograph and jagged paint. Something there felt like relief.

Keeley was leaning on the arm of one of the Adirondack chairs where we sat that night that seemed so long ago now. The heavy sky promised snow and it was sharply cold.

Hey, I said. I leaned down to kiss her. She put her gloved hand on my chest.

I know you need to go to Virginia. And I know none of us quite know how to handle what's going on with Noelle. But I need to know what's happening with you and me.

Whoa. I stepped back. Keeley folded her arms. She blinked her eyes. What do you mean? I asked.

You know what I mean, she said quietly.

Keeley, I said. You know how I feel about you and I want to be supportive but you gotta give me some space, too. My sister, my mom, I want to be able to be there for all of you but you gotta give me a little bit of a break here, Kee.

I'm trying. I want to give you space. But that's not what I'm talking about. She stared at me.

My hands were starting to feel numb. I shoved them in my pockets. I tried to remember the last time I'd seen Keeley outside of school—alone. I couldn't. She knew what I knew, which was that I was avoiding her. That I felt guilty. That I was afraid protecting my sister might mean leaving Keeley. But the problem was, she knew something else too. I thought about the photograph. I thought about the way my sister had just whispered *okay.* I took a few steps closer to Keeley. I took my hands out of my pockets. My fingers were numb with cold. I put them against her icy cheeks.

I'm sorry, I said. She nodded, and my hands moved up and down with her.

Let's just be honest, she said. I know it's gonna be hard, but let's at least do that.

Okay, I said. Here's the thing. I love you. And I don't want you to say anything back. Say it another time, when I don't feel like you're saying it because you have to.

I could feel her smiling as I kissed her.

*　　*　　*

In the morning, Ben picked me up before anyone was awake. It reminded me of the first day of school, when I left the house before anyone was up and everything felt like it was just waking up. This time, everyone in my house was still sleeping but now the morning was dark, and the air was sharp with cold and frost spider-webbed on the windows.

The inside of his van was warm and smelled like coffee.

Newspapers littered the floor and back seat. There were two other volunteers with him—Kevin and Silas. Both of them were actual construction workers. I wasn't sure what I was doing there.

Get in, son, it's cold out there, Ben said.

Talk radio whispered.

Ben looked sideways at me as he backed out of the driveway. I'd told him that my sister wasn't doing well. I didn't tell him any more, but who knows.

Kevin and Silas nodded hello.

We appreciate you coming along, son. I know it's not the time of year for outdoor work but this family'll sure appreciate your help.

I'm happy to do it, I said. I need some distraction.

We drove in silence. It was easy to be silent with Ben. Something about him let you forget he was there, and then he coaxed the words out of you right when you needed them to be coaxed. Kevin and Silas seemed to whisper when they spoke, which was hardly at all.

The house was covered in plastic, big sheets of plastic

that tented out over the half-built structure. There were just the four of us there but I was the only one who had no idea what he was doing. Mostly I just hauled trash from the house site to someone's truck. I used a hammer and pulled nails out of old boards, I tossed the boards into the back of the truck. Sometimes I drove the truck to the dump and unloaded it there.

It was still cold but not as cold as at home. The mountains were full and blue-green. We were sleeping on cots in the office of the church, a drafty, high-ceilinged room. Ben and Kevin woke up early and made eggs and bacon and muffins and we ate while the sun came up over the church. It felt really good to be around people who were quiet and busy and determined. There was nothing else there. We were just trying to repair this house so a family could move back in by Christmas. Period.

On the third and last day, the family stopped by. They drove a station wagon that probably used to be white but was now kind of gray and rusted and filmy. It was a mom and a boy and three girls; they all looked younger than about eight. They piled out of the station wagon, running and tumbling. They all looked sort of square and hard and sad, like the pictures on the cover of *The*

Grapes of Wrath, only in partial color. Their clothes were worn and layered. The mom walked over to me. She was wearing a thick blue plaid jacket. I was the only one out front, tossing the last load of debris into the back of the truck. She held out her hand.

I'm Anna Lowry, she said.

I took her hand.

Nadio Carter, I said.
Thank you.

She was holding a basket over her arm. An actual picnic basket covered in a towel.

I brought y'all some lunch. She dropped my hand. It just really means a lot, what you're doing here.

She gestured around her. The kids had spread—running, chasing, it almost looked like they had multiplied. One of the girls, the youngest probably, clung to her mother's leg.

We're happy to help, I said.

Anna shifted the basket, absently patting her daughter's head.

I've known Ben for a long time, she said. When he moved away we stayed in touch. He's always been a big help to me.

Me too, I said.

Anna smiled.

It's just me and the kids, so I just really appreciate this. The fire was a shock. I could never have done all of this on my own.

Sure, I said again. We're really happy to help you. I didn't know what else to say. She looked so gaunt and sad and the kids took up so much space. She seemed to want me to say something else.

My mom raised us on her own, I said.

Anna continued to smile.

I mean, I know how hard it is.

Just then Ben came around the side of the house. Anna's smile broke across her face. The kids ran to him. Anna walked slowly toward him. They laughed while the kids crowded around his legs.

Family happens in ways that have nothing to do with what we're born into. We think it's supposed to be mom and dad and brother and sister and house and car and high school and summer camp and college and career. I think that isn't how it is anymore. I think mom and dad and brother and sister is the exception and not the rule. And sometimes the pastor at the soup kitchen or the neighbor fills a role that is just as important as blood. I think we mess up somewhere between high school and career and get terrified and become another person, and then another person again.

My sister is the other half of me. I hadn't really let myself think about what would have happened—about the possibility of being a twin without a twin. Anna Lowry and Lace were moms without husbands and we were kids without dads and Keeley was a sister without a brother. But Noelle and I wouldn't be—you can't be a twin without a twin. I felt it in my stomach right there, and for the rest of the day as we finished the house, and all night, awake, as we drove north back home, I felt it until we got home and Ben dropped me off just as the sun was coming up. I'd felt just a glimpse of being one half without the other.

Family isn't what I thought it was at all.

Noelle

I have to do something and I want you guys to come with me.

What, Keeley said. She looked scared.

Nadio stared at me.

We were in the kitchen. It was Saturday morning and almost spring—warm enough that we'd just gone on our Snake Mountain hike, but cold enough that Nadio was holding his hands near the burner where he was boiling water for tea.

I wanna get a tattoo.
You're crazy. Nadio turned back to the stove.
Okay, Keeley said.

Nadio looked back.

> You'll come with me? I asked.
> Yeah, she said. Of course. And Nadio will too.
> I'll come, he said. But you're both crazy.

I hadn't gone back to school. The more days that passed, the farther away it became. I had a social worker I started to see, Christa. At first she was sort of adamant that I go back, but Lace and I were doing assignments at home and I had a tutor for Chemistry and a special home-school agreement and I was doing really well on exams. The idea of the classrooms and hallways felt sort of impossible. And then Christa looked everything over and realized I was okay. And anyway, I promised I'd go back for my senior year. I just felt like I had to figure this new person out—who I was.

In the afternoons Keeley would come over, or I'd sit with Nadio or both of them and they'd go over assignments with me. Once it got warm, we sat on the porch and they told me about what was happening at school, how Jessica Marino was kind of crazy and no one really wanted to be around her (she looks bad, Nadio said, like messed up). They told me about Model U.N. and how maybe next year they'd get the school to host a conference. I didn't really care about Model U.N. but I liked to hear about it. It felt normal. Keeley and I were okay. My brother and I were okay. And I was okay with them, now. Everything was different, and sometimes I felt so lonely it made my chest hurt, like I was sitting on the fringes of everything. But other times I felt like I had this strength that they had no idea about.

There is a certain strength in being alone.

I felt like something was missing though, like I needed one last thing to start this new self. Sometimes Parker's tattoos would show up in my dreams; never his face, never any more of him really, but the lines and curves and shapes of his tattoos, and all of the stories there on his skin. I couldn't stop thinking about them—all beautifully out there and perfectly engraved.

I needed my own.

I knew exactly what I wanted to get. It was a quote from a book Lace always used to read to us. It would be a reminder, like my journal, only on my skin.

Nadio

Noelle was quiet in the car. Keeley drove. I sat in the back seat. I watched the back of their heads. Black and gold and still. Noelle kept reaching behind her, tentatively touching the bandage that peeked out above the neck of her sweater. She'd asked me to go into the room with her at the tattoo place. They'd only let one person in with her. Keeley was sitting in one of the leather chairs, holding a binder spilling out pictures of tattooed strangers.

I'll wait here, she said.

The tattoo artist looked at me. He was stooped over, tall with a long gray beard.

Well? he said.

I followed my sister into the room. She took off her sweater and laid down on the weird tattoo chair. The bearded guy looked down at the piece of paper Noelle had handed him. They whispered more to each other. I felt a little nauseous.

Over here, he said to me.

There were two stools on either side of Noelle. He sat in one. I sat in the other one.

Hey, Noelle said.
Are you nervous?
No, she said. Are you?
Yeah.

I looked at the bearded guy. He was messing with a few bottles and something that looked like a drill. I decided to look at my sister instead. She reached out for my hand.

For a long time there was the buzz of the needle and the grip of Noelle's hand. I stared at her white knuckles. Her eyes were closed. I gripped her hand back. I closed my eyes too.

Nothing can be normal the way we once thought of normal, but these last few months had felt right. The three of us had found our footing. My sister lost her anger. But she'd become distant too. As if all of this had forced her to give less out. Even here in this chair, gripping my hand, I could feel that her strength was bigger than all of ours, and I could feel that part of that was everything she didn't say out loud. She'd never say *that really hurt*. She'd just bite her lip and grip my hand.

All right, he said.

I opened my eyes. It was hard to tell if it had been five minutes or forty. Noelle opened her eyes. They were red and tears smudged the side of her face.

Well? he said.

I looked at my sister's back. Just above the line of her tank top, in small black letters, her skin said,

I remain
Mistress of mine own self
and mine own soul

You like it? Noelle asked. She was watching me.

I knew the quote. When we were growing up, Lace used

to read us *The Foresters* by Tennyson. I was never convinced of Robin Hood as a hero, but Noelle always liked Marian. Read her again, she'd beg Lace. She liked to see Marian stand up to the villains.

Yeah, I said. It's a good thing.

Now in the car, she suddenly seemed older. She and Keeley both seemed, as I watched them from the back seat, like they'd stepped into a new part in their lives. In front of them the road wove gray, signs of spring on both sides. The ever-familiar, bike-worn, foot-worn road. Noelle reached over and switched on the radio. She turned the dial. A hum of static.

Wait, Keeley said. Go back.

Static rolled backwards, and then Noelle's hand stopped on the dial.

Something familiar. A song Lace used to play over and over when we were kids. The rhythm of it, less than the words, rolled a slide show of memories into all of our heads. The day rushed by outside the window. The song rolled louder, filling the car, remembering out loud.

Noelle and Keeley laughed into the lyrics. I cracked the

window, sticking my arm out. The air was almost warm. Noelle and Keeley were singing. I rolled the window all the way down. Their voices got louder.

*   *   *

Dear Dario,

I'm done with all of this. This is going to be my last letter. I think part of me thought I needed you so I could get through all of this. I wondered if I could write through what you might tell me. But I actually never needed you.

Lace keeps a real eye on us now. She's been teaching Noelle from home all semester and working on top of that. She's been doing the job of mom and dad and teacher now. For every space you left empty, she's trying to fill it twice.

Noelle is okay. She's going to go back to school in the fall. She got a tattoo, which I really don't understand. But it was important to her. And she got a job baking. She bakes all of the time. She feels really good about creating things and I think she likes that the results of her baking sort of please people. She and I were always very different in school. We were both fine—but Noelle was never very into any one thing. Maybe baking is her thing. I don't know how you did in school. Lace is always telling me she was never as smart as I am—that she doesn't know where it came from. I know I care about history and I care about the rights of people whose government isn't supporting them. I know I want to do something that helps people who can't really raise their voice. I don't think I got this from you because I'm pretty certain you don't care about anything but yourself.

Noelle and I are going to be seventeen soon. You and Lace were seventeen when you met. This is hard to imagine. But I realize that you probably couldn't have been in love with her. You didn't know what that meant. You're not capable. And I'm fine with that right now. Because I know now I love Keeley. And we are pretty young and we might break up one day because our lives go in different directions or things change, but even then, I'd never be able to just walk out on her. Even then I'd always know I loved her right now.

What I've learned without ever knowing you is that I'm nothing like you.

I didn't know what kind of man I could be when this whole year started. I thought maybe that was because I'd never had a dad. But I think that is exactly why I know what kind of man to be. Just this one—who is about to start track season and is thinking about going to Princeton and wants to take his girlfriend to see the house he built in

Virginia and is going to cook dinner tonight so his mom doesn't have to and can't wait to try the pear tart his sister is bringing home from work.

That's who I am.

Noelle

When I was with Parker, I used to pretend to fall asleep for the feeling I'd get when he watched me with my eyes closed. That spring, I started to sleep so hard. Keeley was right. I didn't stop thinking about him, but it lessened.

I started working in a bakery, too. I really like it. I can't get rid of this idea that making food is an art in its own way. I have no idea what I want to do, but I love the smell of sugar and apples. I love adding the wrong spice to something and seeing if it works. I love kneading cold floury dough over and over with my knuckles. I love handing someone a box of frosted vanilla cupcakes, being a part of their secret guilty pleasure.

The thing about a bakery is, you have to get there really early in the morning, like five o'clock, before the sun comes up. But I have my license now, so I drive. I have to park in a lot across the street, and that is where I saw him.

It was so early in the morning it was still dark out. Even though the bakery is on Division street, which has all kinds of shops and restaurants, nothing was open yet. I was crossing the deserted street when I saw him, the outline of him really, coming down the street. His hands in his pockets, his bony elbows angled out, his faded jeans loose and baggy. I had the bakery keys in my hand, shaking. He must have been coming from a party somewhere. I knew he'd been up all night.

We were standing in front of each other on the dark sidewalk. His eyes wide.

Whoa, he said. Hi.
Hi.
What are you ... he stopped. He hugged me. I could feel his heart beating into my forehead.
I work here. I gestured at the bakery window. He looked up at the bakery but I don't think he saw it. He looked back at me. His eyes were watery. He was drunk.

How … he looked around. He put his hand on my elbow and nodded toward the bench in front of the bakery.

Can you sit down a minute?

I checked my watch, pretending time was important. I knew no one else would be arriving for another half an hour. I knew I had to sit down.

Okay.

We sat down. Parker put his hands over his face and rubbed his eyes. Then he looked up.

Listen, Noelle, I …

I realized just then that I had no idea if he knew what had happened, if he knew I'd been in the hospital, or if he just thought we broke up. I didn't want to know.

It's okay, I said.

No. I'm just … you're a really incredible girl and I shouldn't have—

Seriously. It's okay.

He looked at his lap, then at me.

No, he said. It's not all okay. I wasn't good to you.

230

You were so honest all the time and I just, you know, I should have been better to you.

I took a deep breath. It felt so strange to see myself through him. I realized I had always wanted this regret from him. For everything I remembered and tried not to, that regret was what I wanted.

Then I thought of something.

> Can you take your jacket off? I asked.
> What?
> Please.

He looked at me for another long second, then he shrugged out of his jacket. I took his arm in my hands. I suddenly felt so strong, holding his arm, my finger tips just barely touching the skin.

> I remember this tattoo, I said to him, but it doesn't look like I remembered it. I pulled back the sleeve of his T-shirt and looked from his shoulder to his wrist.
> And this one...
> Yeah, he said.

There was something else there now, deep colors and fuller designs reaching to the crook of his elbow.

He looked down now at the bend of his wrist.

I had it filled in, he said. This one I had filled in.
I remembered it different, I thought out loud.

He looked at my hand holding his arm.

I'd remembered it all different—the shape and stretch of these tattoos that now seemed to fill in all the places on once-familiar skin. And in their shapes and colors lay none of the designs I remembered and everything I wanted to see.

The tattoo I remembered best was the serpent that wound up the inside of his forearm, from wrist to the crook of his elbow. That first night, it was the most beautiful thing I'd ever seen. But later, I thought maybe I'd seen it in a movie and not on this skin—there is nothing like it there now, just a twisting blend of colors, just a spread and mesh of designs. But something I do remember, something that is still there, is the dirt under his fingernails—the dirt of the kitchen where he works still, the grease from the kitchen hood and the remnants of dishes he cooked for someone else, the food they swallowed with sighs and whispered about later, the taste they still remember today while never knowing the shape of the tattoos on these arms, the shapes I should remember but can't because they've changed.

I thought about Keeley and what she said to me in my room.

What? Parker said into the silence.

We come back to the same people to learn something about how we have changed. We want to be assured that we have changed. We so want our pictures to paint differently than they do.

But I didn't say any of this out loud.

I have to go, I said, dropping his arm into his lap. I stood up.

Noelle—

It's good to see you, I said. It really is. But I have to go.

He was sitting there as I walked around to the back door of the bakery. I think he watched me walk away. But when I went into the store and turned on the lights and looked out at the bench, he was gone, and the sun was coming up and the street was gray-pink and deserted.

©Hillery Stone

About the Author

Heather Duffy Stone writes stories and essays that are mostly inspired by high school—either her own or someone else's. *This Is What I Want to Tell You* is her first novel. She has lived in Vermont, England, Los Angeles, rural New York, and Rome, Italy. For now she cooks, sleeps, explores, writes, and teaches in Brooklyn, New York.